LURE
OF THE
PRAYING
MANTIS

DAVID GASTON

BALBOA.PRESS
A DIVISION OF HAY HOUSE

Balboa Press books may be ordered through booksellers or by contacting:

Balboa Press
A Division of Hay House
1663 Liberty Drive
Bloomington, IN 47403
www.balboapress.co.uk
UK TFN: 0800 0148647 (Toll Free inside the UK)
UK Local: (02) 0369 56325 (+44 20 3695 6325 from outside the UK)

Print information available on the last page.

ISBN: 978-1-9822-8650-7 (sc)
ISBN: 978-1-9822-8651-4 (e)

Balboa Press rev. date: 10/26/2022

CHAPTER
ONE

★ ★ ★ ★

She was born plain old Ann, without the 'e', Walker. But she wanted something classier, so she added the 'e', then a hyphen, and then her best friend's name, 'Marie'. And Walker had to go too, especially after her mother had told her the origins of the name. One of her ancestors had once 'walked the wool' in a fulling mill, spending hours treading raw wool into a smelly solution contained in a large vat. That 'smelly solution' had been raw urine. *No,* she had thought with contempt, *that name has got to go. How about winter?* she had thought. *That sounds classy, especially if the 'i' is turned into a 'y', and how about putting 'De' before it? Yes,* she had thought with deep satisfaction, *I like that.* So, when she moved into a house of her own in an area of Bellingham Borough where nobody knew her; the tall, curvaceous, self-confident, and manipulative woman changed her name from Ann Walker to Anne-Marie De Wynter.

Men were her target, and her sexuality was her weapon. Anne-Marie was attractive, although she could never be considered an entrant for a beauty contest. Her blond hair was shoulder length and curly, her face was round with blue eyes and an engaging smile. Anne-Marie ate frugally so that her ample charms remained deliciously ample rather than overpoweringly ample. She knew what men liked and so she dressed and behaved as though she would offer it all, but without giving anything. Life is all about give and take; well men would give, and Anne-Marie would take.

Men found her sexually attractive, and Anne-Marie knew it. This was the source of her power, and she used it mercilessly. She was in command, always in command. She would psychologically castrate them by degrading their names into an effeminate, almost childlike, form. So, Michael became Mickey, Timothy became Timmy, and William became Willy. She dominated them like a mother figure, making them do things that they otherwise would not want to do.

It was a game. She had learnt it in school, but not from her teachers. When she lifted her skirt behind the bike shed, she would study the excited looks on the boys' faces as eagerly as they studied her exposed knickers.' Knowledge is power', a teacher had once told her. How right he was; knowing the boys' interest in her sexuality was power, and it could be used to her advantage. But it was not just the financial gains that could be made, and she had made a few, it was the control that she enjoyed. Anne-Marie liked, even loved, the power of domination and control that she could exert over members of the other sex.

But as she stood in the modestly furnished lounge of Jack's flat, her face was as white and cold as snow. Jack Manning was nearly fifty years of age, twice Anne-Marie's age, a friend, a very good friend. He had helped her to get a personal assistant's position with a local managing director of a small firm, even to the point of giving her a reference. And she had rewarded him by including him in one of her games, although he had participated unwittingly. And now he lay on the pale green carpet, blood oozing from a smashed skull. The weapon, a heavily blood-stained black handled hammer, lay by his side.

This was something new; something that she had never witnessed before. She was shocked, naturally, Anne-Marie had never seen a dead body before, and even though she had prepared herself mentally for this moment, the sight of Jack's life blood forming a bright red halo around his head was still a jolt to her system. Fortunately, she had worn her brown gloves because of the cold autumn breeze that was blowing outside; they would prevent any of her fingerprints from being left in the flat.

Anne-Marie stood in a state of numbness at the sight of Jack's body, but she did not cry. She never cried; unless it was in a worthy cause; her own.

She allowed her eyes to wander around the room. She saw how neat and tidy it was; A place for everything and everything in its place; that was one of Jack's favourite sayings. His numerous chess books were filed alphabetically both in the bookcase and on the shelf under the glass-topped coffee table. A computer, its screen displaying a blue and white chequered chess board, was on a bridge table in the corner, with the attached printer sitting on the floor underneath. But her eyes settled on Jack's pride and joy; the coin collection resting proudly in its blue velvet case lying within the pine wood display cabinet. The lid was up allowing the viewer to see the gold and silver coins reclining in their regimented rows as though on parade. Slowly, and without a second glance at Jack's prostrate form, Anne-Marie crossed the room to the cabinet, withdrew the case, closed the lid, and hid it from sight beneath the brown calf length leather coat that she wore. She was about to turn to depart when the corners of her mouth creased up in a slight smile. Her gloved hand reached into the cabinet and withdrew a small, inscribed silver charm bracelet with several charms, including a rabbit's foot and a gold heart, hanging from it. She pushed the bracelet into her coat pocket. Anne-Marie touched nothing else within the cabinet.

The sunlight was disappearing into the cold evening air as Anne-Marie emerged into the busy street below Jack's flat. She glanced at the window of the hardware shop; the owner of which was Jack's landlord who rented him the upstairs flat above his place of business. The shop was in darkness with the windows shuttered and padlocked. So were some of the other shops as well, except for the mini-market and the chemist.

Anne-Marie mixed with the people hurrying home; hoping no one would recognize her. But why should they? She very rarely came to this part of town, and when she did it was usually at night to visit Jack. And the throng of people that she was in would be more interested in getting home to their evening meals than in her.

Benny's car, an old light blue Nissan with a dented passenger door, was in the library car park. Anne-Marie, without looking around her, as she did not want to attract attention to herself, unlocked the driver's door and slid calmly behind the steering wheel. The car's engine purred into life; hardly raising a decibel as she engaged first gear and drove calmly off the car park and into the bustling traffic moving towards the suburbs.

Jimmy was on holiday in Tunisia, but Anne-Marie knew where he hid the key to his allotment shed. She walked through the dark and deserted communal allotments towards Jimmy's shed, a well maintained and pleasantly decorated blue and white wooden structure. Keeping her gloves on, she withdrew the key from its hiding place beneath the plant pot on the windowsill and opened the shed door. A comfortable armchair, heating stove, and a small wooden cabinet containing Jimmy's tea making utensils where on one side of the one roomed building, whilst plant pots and gardening tools littered the other side both on the floor and on soil-stained wooden shelves. Anne-Marie placed the velvet case on the floor in the corner amongst some tools and covered it with a dirty mud splattered blanket. She then left via the same route that she had used to arrive.

As she sat once again in the light blue Nissan, she reached into her pocket and withdrew the charm bracelet. Anne-Marie smiled as she read the inscription; '*To my beloved Cathy*'. The smile soon disappeared along with the bracelet which Anne-Marie placed out of sight under the passenger seat.

It was a quarter to seven by her expensively styled watch, a Christmas present from Jimmy, as she turned slowly into the car park of Belvedere Gardens, an over-elaborate name for a collection of concrete maisonettes. The car park was no more than a courtyard surrounded by several towers, each of three stories. Ann-Marie pulled into a vacant parking space in front of the second tower.

Benny was waiting for her. She waved to him as she climbed demurely out of the car. He did not wave back.

With an anxious look, and a nervous twitch of his shoulders, Benny hurriedly entered the second story maisonette, leaving the front door open for Anne-Marie. As she climbed the concrete steps leading to Benny's front door a broad smile beamed from her face; it was a smile of success. Her thoughts were of '*I'm going to get away with this.*'

CHAPTER
TWO

★ ★ ★ ★

Detective Inspector James Buchan was a boring man; at least that was how his wife described him, even up to the point when she divorced him four years ago. But he did not regard himself as boring at all; single minded perhaps, but not boring. He did concede the point though that his life was his work; unfortunately, his wife did not share his enthusiasm for police work. Divorce was inevitable once his two daughters had left home for university.

He pulled up outside the hardware shop having just left one of his daughters, Becky, at home crying over a broken relationship. That was not an area of his that he could call a speciality; his ex-wife, Jacqueline, on the other hand, was an expert. It was a point that he had reminded her of frequently, especially during their divorce proceedings. Now he only saw his daughters as they moved from one parent to the other. His elder daughter, Helen, but maybe more so Becky, had tried and failed on several occasions to get them back together. James could only smile at the suggestion; Jacqueline was out of his life forever.

D.I. Buchan hurried up the stairs, leaping two steps at a time, and stopped, only slightly breathless, at the front door of Jack Manning's flat. The young constable at the door opened it to allow him to enter.

Detective Sergeant Daisy Durham, 'Daye' to her friends because she hated the name Daisy, had her long, and curly, jet-black hair tied back in a ponytail to make her younger looking than her thirty years. But her delicate features, although black and beautiful which betrayed her West Indian origins, also betrayed a mature and knowledgeable look that showed that she was experienced in the world. She was stood in the hallway talking to a uniformed constable as D.I. Buchan entered. She dismissed him before turning to face her superior.

'Morning, Sir.' She greeted blandly, withdrawing her notebook from the breast pocket of her navy-blue trouser suit.

James looked at his sergeant; she was too much like Jacqueline. It was not so much the physical side of her that reminded him, although Daye Durham and Jacqueline are both of slim build, had attractive elf like faces with penetratingly chestnut brown eyes. They both even had black hair, but which Jacqueline preferred to be cut shorter than Daye's. Their similarity of character also attracted James' attention; Daye had a calm, thoughtful, almost analytical, brain with the ability to sift information and to even categorise such knowledge. Jacqueline could do the same, but only with knowledge that she could use in quiz shows. Police work, or indeed anything connected with crime or violence, held no interest for her whatsoever. But James had loved her in the beginning, and she had given him two beautiful daughters, but apart from that he believed that he should never have married her.

'What have we got, sergeant?' James demanded with authority; his voice gruff with a faint trace of a Scottish accent which betrayed his origins before he moved to a force in a Northern English town.

'Jack Manning,' Daye began, reading from her notebook, 'Forty-eight, widower, lived alone. Someone caved his skull in with a hammer. That is being checked now by forensics.'

'Was it one blow or repeated blows?'

'It was definitely a frenzied attack, Sir.' Daye continued. 'Probably three days ago.'

James stroked his closely shaven chin as he listened.

'Any sign of a forced entry?'

'No, Sir. The victim must have let his killer in.'

'Who found the body?'

'Ms Pat Conway, the victim's sister. Jack Manning was in the habit of going for a newspaper before breakfast every day. The last morning, he did that was last Tuesday. When Ms Conway saw the newsagent this morning and was told that Jack had not collected his paper for three days; she came round to see what was wrong with her brother. She's in the kitchen.'

James looked towards the closed door and imagined the woman that was beyond it. He could only guess what must have passed through her mind having found her brother murdered. But first he would investigate the lounge.

Jack Manning's covered body lay on a stretcher on the floor awaiting removal to the local mortuary where it could be examined more thoroughly. The bright red halo, stark against the pale green of the carpet, was the only sign that something was wrong, although the double door to the display cabinet was slightly ajar.

'That's the only item that appears to have been touched.' Daye informed her boss, pointing a long index finger towards the pine wood piece of furniture.

James slowly approached it. Several silver, and expensive looking, plates and goblets lay untouched on their glass shelves. There they sat, highly polished and uniform; so much so that James could clearly see himself on their shiny surfaces. *Did his face really look so ingrained and lived in as that?* He thought to himself; and then smiled as he thought '*yes*' to his own question. He was now mid-forties, nearly six feet in height, but without a 'beer belly' that some men of his age were apt to get as they approached middle age. James was broad but not fat. He liked to keep fit although he did not have the time to work out at a gymnasium.

'They look valuable,' Daye said quietly. 'And yet they have been left.'

'Something was taken.' James said firmly, nodding his dark-haired head with the greying temples towards the large space on the middle shelf. 'Maybe Ms Conway can tell us what should be there.'

Pat Conway, her tear-stained face buried in a handkerchief, was sat at the table as D.I. Buchan and D.S. Durham entered the kitchen. The young female officer with her stood to attention as her superior officers entered but retook her seat as James motioned with his hand for her to sit down again. James also sat down at the table, directly opposite Ms Conway, while Daye stood beside the door, pencil and notebook in hand, ready to make notes.

'I'm so sorry, Ms Conway.' James began sincerely, his voice deliberately soft and calming, 'but I have to ask you certain questions but only if you feel up to it.'

Pat Conway withdrew the handkerchief from her face and held it tightly in a ball between her two clenched hands. Her eyes were red and yet defiant; she lifted her head proudly and stared directly into James' blue green eyes. For a moment she nodded her short cropped dark-haired head in a silent answer to the D.I.'s question. James immediately admired her.

'Can I ask you when you last saw your brother?'

'It was last weekend.' She answered quickly, trying to hold back the sobs that were obviously welling up inside of her.

'How did he seem to you?' James asked quietly, as though trying to gently prompt an answer from her. 'Did he seem worried or concerned about anything?'

'No. He had just been to some coin fair in Manchester. He had finally managed to get hold of an Edward the First silver penny in mint condition. He needed one for his collection. Now he had one he was as happy as a man who had just won the lottery.'

'Where did he keep his coin collection, Ms Conway?'

Pat Conway was trying to look brave. At James' question tears suddenly began to flow down her reddened cheeks.

'Don't say it has gone.'

'Was it in the display cabinet?'

'O God. It's not there is it?'

James nodded slightly, averting his eyes from the piercing look of Pat Conway.

'What can you tell us about the coin collection?' he eventually asked, his eyes now staring intently at Pat Conway's round, and in his opinion, attractive face.

Ms Conway did not reply immediately.

'If you could give us a description, please, Ms Conway.' It was the soft dulcet tones of Daye that encouraged her. 'It could help us to find the person responsible for this attack on your brother.'

Only slowly did the tears stop flowing.

'They were in a blue velvet case.' She began, her voice faltering between sobs. 'There were gold and silver coins in it. One was a Charles the First silver half crown, A silver sixpence from the time of Elizabeth the First, Gold sovereigns from the time of Queen Victoria, plus some other coins that I cannot remember including some from the present Queen Elizabeth.'

'Would the Edward the First coin that you mentioned...?'

'You mean the silver penny?'

'Yes.' James continued. 'Would that be in the case?'

'Most certainly,' Pat said with half a smile on her face. 'That would have been the first thing that Jack did when he got home.'

'Could you put a price on this collection?' James asked warily, adding quickly. 'It could help us to find it.'

'A few thousand,' Pat answered quietly, as though the value of the collection was unimportant and insignificant, which it was against the value of a life. 'I think it was insured for seven or eight thousand pounds, but I'm not sure.'

'Did many people know of this collection?'

'Of course,' Pat answered softly. 'Jack was immensely proud of it. He would have showed it off to anyone that visited.'

'Did he get many visitors?'

'A few,' she answered solemnly. 'I only wish I knew their names.'

James cut short the interview. There was nothing more to be gleaned from the victim's sister, well not at this time anyway. If Jack Manning were as proud of the coin collection as Pat Conway had said, then just about any visitor to the flat could be called a suspect. It was little to go on.

'Check all likely coin dealers in the area.' He ordered Daye as he was about to depart from the flat. 'It sounds very distinctive; somebody may just recognise it.'

'OK, Sir.'

'And check with the locals about Tuesday. Somebody may just remember a visitor on that day.'

'Yes, Sir.'

James Buchan looked at Daye Durham; she was efficient and orderly. He had thought about asking her out for a meal but had then told himself that his life was complicated enough without complicating matters at work as well. *No*, he told himself firmly, *get back home where you belong; get back home to your own lonely existence.*

CHAPTER
THREE

Anne-Marie De Wynter, both hands over her mouth and her eyes wide open, stood in apparent shock beside the mock open log fire. Sat in the reclining chair in front of her was Pat Conway, tears rolling freely down her cheeks as she told Anne-Marie of the previous day's events.

'But why, Jack?' Anne-Marie blurted. 'He wouldn't have harmed a fly.'

Pat Conway did not answer immediately; she was obviously still in shock and seemed to struggle to comprehend anything that had happened yesterday.

But Anne-Marie knew what had happened, although she was not going to admit to anything.

'They took his coin collection.' Pat said slowly, the tone of her voice tinged with sadness and regret, 'even a charm bracelet with little value. Why take that?'

Anne-Marie looked at Pat. She felt sorry for her, in a way, but she supposed this was what was meant by 'collateral damage'. Only Jack was to be physically hurt, but Jack's family was being mentally hurt. *That was unfortunate*, thought Anne-Marie, *but it could not be avoided*.

'I asked John to check the display cabinet.' Pat added, referring to her husband. 'I just could not do it. But all they took were his coins and a bracelet belonging to Cathy. Nothing else was taken, not even those silver goblets and they must be worth a small fortune. Why leave them?'

'Could they have been disturbed do you think?' Anne-Marie offered, slowly walking the length of the modestly furnished lounge of her nineteen thirties style semi-detached home in the Belmont district of town. 'Otherwise, those items would've been taken as well, wouldn't they?'

Pat nervously shrugged her shoulders as though she could not be bothered to even think about the question let alone answer it. Slumped in the recliner, eyes red from continuous crying, Pat Conway was a vision of utter despair, struggling to come to terms with the murder of her younger brother. Her husband had told most of the family members what had happened to Jack, but she had to tell Anne-Marie herself.

This was exactly what Anne-Marie had expected. She was not a relative, of course, but Jack had known her from childhood; indeed, she had called him Uncle Jack from the time that she could begin speaking. He had been her father's best friend, and when he had died in a road accident almost twenty years ago, Jack, naturally, took over the role of substitute father to Ann; a role that Ann had been happy for him to do; At least until she had established herself as an independent person with a mind of her own and knew where she wanted to go in life. That destiny would not include Jack Manning.

'I'm grateful you came to tell me yourself.' Anne-Marie told Pat, looking out of the spacious bay window overlooking the throng of people hurrying back and forth doing; well, whatever they chose to do on a fine Saturday morning. 'I know it cannot have been easy for you.'

Pat did not reply. Another flood of tears, suddenly and without warning, cascaded down her cheeks. Anne-Marie went to her with words of comfort and compassion, the image of the family friend filled with sympathy and love for her Uncle Jack. But as she embraced Pat, the distraught sister could not possibly see the ends of Anne-Marie's full lipped mouth curl up into a slight sinister smile of satisfaction.

What had made Anne-Marie so callous and deceitful? Maybe Anne-Marie herself could not be sure of the reason. The Walker family had not been poor; working class certainly, but never poor. Her father had always tried to better himself although with limited success. He had taught Ann the value of ambition; to always strive to be the best in everything that she did. She had tried, using honesty as her main weapon, to be the best, first at school and then at the athletics track, but Ann had also met with only limited success. But she had one advantage over her father, Ann was a girl. Those days behind the bike shed had brought her some rewards, like Tommy Spence doing her geography homework in exchange for a 'feel'; Joshua Anderson stealing the France holiday trip money from Miss Jepson's desk because Ann wanted to buy the latest single from Oasis; a task which Joshua did for only a kiss; a reward which Ann did not give because she found Joshua Anderson so repulsive. Anne-Marie always smiled when she thought of Joshua Anderson; she not only bought the Oasis single but had money left over for a hundred more singles. And as for poor Joshua, he not only did not get a kiss from Ann, but he was also eventually unmasked as the thief and excluded from school. His hoped-for career as a doctor lay in ruins; he never went to university, never studied medicine, and ended his education in one of her majesty's prisons after a betting shop fraud went wrong.

Poor Joshua Anderson, Anne-Marie would often think to herself, *Poor bloody fool*!!!! It was a thought which Anne-Marie always followed with a sarcastic laugh.

There were other minor successes; Phil Green managed to steal and photocopy the Maths exam paper; one copy he kept for himself, the other one for Ann. His reward was to be able to 'go all the way' with Ann. She promised that she would on the first Saturday after the exam; there was to be a party at Marie's house to celebrate the end of term exams. Unfortunately for Phil, however, was the fact that he was caught cheating at the exam and was then banned from attending any parties for a year by his rather angry parents. The teachers never said what had led them to suspect that Phil was cheating, but it was rumoured at the time that the teachers had been alerted to the possibility of cheating by an anonymous phone call. The phone caller was never traced.

Only rarely did Ann keep her promises and that was only if it was unavoidable. But she soon learnt how to avoid them. Like with young Frank Dawes who was promised a date if he stole some perfume from local cosmetics shop for her. Young Frank did as he was asked, gave Ann the perfume, and then waited for his reward. Ann told him to continue stealing for her; if he refused, she would inform on him to the police. Frank was frightened but did as he was told. For over a year young Frank was blackmailed to steal for Ann; he never went out on a date with her.

Why was dishonesty more successful for Anne-Marie than honesty? Mind you the sense of danger and the thrill of power held a fatal attraction for her. And it was more fun. She enjoyed it.

'I'll let you know the funeral arrangements when I find out myself.' Pat cried in Anne-Marie's ear. 'But I've got to wait for the body to be released first.'

Anne-Marie nodded solemnly.

'I suppose there must be an autopsy?' she asked with a slight grimace on her face as though the very thought of it was repugnant.

'Yes.' Pat answered through her tears. 'But I hope we can lay him to rest soon.'

'Have the police said much?' Anne-Marie prompted. 'Who's leading the investigation for example?'

'Some Detective Inspector somebody or other,' Pat replied, shaking her head as though desperately trying to remember. 'Buchan, I think he is called, Detective Inspector Buchan. Seems nice enough but..................'

Pat allowed her voice to tail off as though unsure how to end the sentence. But Anne-Marie nodded her reassurance as though she understood.

It was time for Pat to leave. Anne-Marie helped her on with her old grey coat and led her to the door. John was waiting in the old Cortina outside. Pat had told him to stay outside as she had wanted to talk to Anne-Marie alone. She waved to him as she opened the front door for Pat; he returned the wave as he got out of the car to rush to help his wife. John was tall and thin, had little hair, which was all grey, and had a permanent solemn expression, ideal for the unfortunate events of yesterday.

As he led Pat to the car he smiled at Anne-Marie but said nothing. There was nothing to say. Pat walked like a zombie allowing herself to be led by John. Anne-Marie watched passively as the tall solemn gent helped Pat into the car and slowly drove away with her. As she closed the door Anne-Marie took a deep breath, lent slightly against the wooden back of the door, and smiled.

It was almost like she had received an electric shock the way Anne-Marie suddenly moved from the door, ran up the stairs to her bedroom, and took the small mobile phone from the drawer of her dressing table.

With a steely gaze in her eyes and a resolute expression on her face Anne-Marie calmly dialled 999.

'Emergency, which Service do you require?' An unemotional female voice asked, almost demanded to know.

Anne-Marie placed a handkerchief over the mouthpiece of the phone and spoke in a gruff, almost unintelligible Irish accent, 'police.'

'Police' a male voice said, as unemotional as the first.

'This is for Detective Inspector Buchan. Jack Manning's killer is to be found at the canal side allotment of Jimmy MacGregor. His name is Benny Gordon. He will be there all day. Evidence lies in the allotment shed.'

'Who is this?' The voice demanded to know.

Anne-Marie ended the call. She knew that the message was being recorded so that even if her false Irish accent had been difficult to understand, the police would be able to use playback to decipher her words. Now to dispose of the mobile phone that she had bought only the week before using a false name and address and had never used it until now. *A nice walk along the banks of the Leeds - Liverpool canal sounds inviting,* Anne-Marie thought smugly to herself, *and I'll put the phone and a brick into a plastic bag. They will never find that lying in the mud under twelve feet of water.*

CHAPTER
FOUR

★ ★ ★ ★

Police Headquarters on Templegate was of a modern design; indeed, it had won several design awards. A mixture of concrete, glass, and chrome, surrounded as it was by a well-designed and laid out garden containing a mixture of shrubs and bedding plants, gave the impression of a futuristic building connected with science or high finance rather than one with law enforcement. Indeed, if the large rotating sign next to the concrete steps had not displayed 'Police Divisional Headquarters', the visitor could have been excused for thinking that he had walked into a bank, or the HQ of a pharmaceutical company.

James Buchan's office, however, did not match the exterior. It was spacious enough though; room for six officers; even had computers and printers on desks, and a coffee making machine in the corner. But only two officers occupied the office, himself, and Daye Durham. One other officer was on sick leave whilst the fourth, fifth and sixth desks were unoccupied due to a shortage of staff. This left James desperately searching for replacements to help with an ever-increasing workload; a workload which displayed itself in files and reports scattered on the tops of desks, and some which had fallen off the desktops and onto the floor making the office look very untidy and unprofessional. The cleaners had even complained to him about it. How were they supposed to clean the desks when they could not even see the desktops? They had argued. James had agreed with them, but the files were needed. Each file and report were of an unsolved crime; a crime which he and his team were expected to solve.

Like the thick file that lay opened on the desk in front of him. A below average height man, probably five feet three or four, wearing a dark blue track suit with a matching balaclava, and speaking with a soft local accent had attacked, robbed, and sexually assaulted five women over a five-month period. His MO, his *modus operandi*, had always been the same; wait for his victim, usually a young mother with a child, to leave one of the large superstores in the area carrying her weekly shopping onto the car park. As she struggled with the child and the shopping the masked attacker would grab the child; hold a knife to her throat; it was always a young girl and bundle her into the back of the victim's car whilst ordering the mother to get into the driver's seat. The mother usually obeyed immediately, especially after seeing the fear in her child's eyes and the sharp knife at her throat. He always calmed his victim though by saying that he was escaping from the police and that he just wanted the mother to drive him out of town where mother and daughter would be released unharmed. The end of the journey was usually a quiet wooded area. It was there that the victim was robbed of her money, credit cards, and any jewellery that she may have been wearing including her wristwatch. The victim was then ordered to strip naked. Fearful for her child, for the attacker always kept the knife to the child's throat, the young mother always did as she was told. He would then assault her in a humiliating way; usually with something that was lying close by on the ground such as a can or a broken branch of a tree. The attacker would then steal the woman's car keys, and her clothes, and drive away from the area in her car leaving the woman and child traumatised and degraded.

James shook his head as he read the statements from the victims. What sort of creature gets pleasure from this sort of act? Unfortunately, James had met some of society's dregs during his lengthy career as a police officer. He well knew what depths of depravity the human mind could sink to. It still disgusted him though.

But those five attacks had been four years ago. They had stopped as quickly as they had started, and nothing had been seen or heard of the attacker since then; until two days ago that is.

James looked at the statement of Valerie Clark, twenty-seven years old with a four-year-old daughter, Chloe. It looked so familiar. She had done her shopping at Turner's, the new hyper market on the outskirts of Bellingham. A man, probably five feet three in height and wearing a dark blue track suit with a matching balaclava, had seized her daughter, and put a knife to her throat. The remainder of her statement read just like the other victims' statements. The only difference was that Ms Clark's attacker had used a broken bottle in his attack on her and had left her seriously injured and in agony.

He's getting more vicious, thought James, his disgust now edged with anger as he read of Valerie's injuries. She would require hospital treatment for some considerable time.

But was it the same person? James asked himself, *or was it a copycat? Perhaps someone who had read of the previous attacks in the local paper?* It was possible but unlikely. For not only was the MO of the attack identical to the previous five victims, but, more importantly, the description of the attacker and the fact that he spoke in a soft local accent was identical as well. It had to be the same man. *So why the four years delay between victim number five and victim number six?* James stroked his chin as he pondered on that question.

'Oh. Good morning, Sir.'

James looked up from the file to see a startled expression on Daye Durham's face as she stood in the office doorway.

'I didn't think you'd be in this morning.' Daye continued, closing the door behind her, and approaching her superior's desk. She was holding yet another report in front of her.

'I know it's Saturday, but....' He said dryly using a wave of his hand to finish the sentence as he indicated all the files and reports that littered the office. He then pointed to the report that he was reading. 'And this one is pretty nasty.'

'Valerie Clark.' Daye said sadly, as she quickly recognised it. 'I took that statement myself from her. She's a brave woman but was in a hell of a lot of pain.'

'You weren't here four years ago, were you?'

'No, Sir. I was transferred here just under three years ago. Why do you ask?'

James handed the file that he had been reading over to her. With a thoughtful and painstaking look of intrigue she read the first few pages slowly before raising her brown eyes towards James who had changed his position and now stood beside the open window of his office. He turned towards her.

'Is this the same.........?' Daye began.

'I believe it is.' James interrupted, answering the anticipated question. 'The attack on Valerie Clark is identical to what happened to those five women. I suggest you read up on that file before we proceed any further. He attacked five women over a five-month period, always leaving a few weeks between each attack. If he's back on the prowl, I want him caught before the bastard murders some poor woman. He's obviously getting more dangerous.'

'Yes Sir.' Daye agreed, nodding her head quickly so that her long black hair, now free of the ponytail, cascaded over her shoulders. 'I see that you were the investigating officer at the time.'

James nodded his head but did not answer.

'May I ask if you had any theories about this man?'

It was a fair question, thought James. But what could he give as an answer? All leads just ended up blind alleys, with absolutely no clue as to the man's identity. There was one line of enquiry that he had tried though, although that too had proved fruitless in the end.

'What was the car that Mrs. Clark was driving?'

'A VW Golf 1.4 in metallic pearl, Sir.' Daye answered quickly. 'Although less than two years old, Ms Clark bought it second hand three months ago. I've started all the usual traces for it. If we can find it, we may be able to find this sick pervert.'

'Read the file thoroughly.' James commanded. 'Each of the first five victims had her car stolen as well as Valerie Clark: VW, Toyota, Rover, Volvo, and then another Toyota.

All vehicles were less than two years old. None were ever recovered. What does that suggest to you?'

Daye paused before answering. James knew that she was thinking intently because she always flared her nostrils. It always made James Buchan the man look at Daye Durham the woman; and an extremely attractive woman at that.

'Stolen to order perhaps?' She offered softly, although she did not sound too convincing. 'But that wouldn't account for the attacks on the women though.'

'It might.' James said coldly, turning to face the window so that he could admire the view of the river and the Belmont district beyond with its contrasting styles of pre-world-war two buildings and its modern housing estates all built around a large central park with tree lined roads emanating from it. 'Maybe that is why there is always a few weeks between attacks. He is targeting both the car and the woman.'

Daye flared her nostrils again at the very suggestion that these women were being deliberately targeted. It was obviously not a pleasant thought for her. She was a woman herself after all.

'Is that a new report?' James suddenly asked, pointing to the report that she had in her hand.

'It's the pathology report on Jack Manning.' She answered coldly. 'It confirms what we suspected. Death was caused by multiple fractures of the skull inflicted by that black-handled hammer. The forensics team have some good prints off it and found matching prints on other items in the flat, mainly on the front door and the coffee table.'

'Sounds like he was being rather careless, doesn't it?'

'Yes, Sir.' Agreed Daye but added cautiously 'but careful enough not to be seen either entering or leaving the flat. Enquiries in that direction have drawn a complete blank.'

'Nothing unusual spotted at all?'

'There is one possibility, Sir.' Daye offered tentatively. 'The manageress of the library reports that a light blue Nissan car, model and licence number unknown, was seen parked on the library car park twice on that day; once in the morning and once in the afternoon.'

'What's the significance of that?'

'It is only a small car park and only people using the library are supposed to park there. In fact, it is only a small library. Two people employed there. The manageress knows most of the people that use the library and none of them own a light blue Nissan.'

'Could be someone using a nearby shop.' James offered thoughtfully to which Daye merely shrugged her shoulders as though she had to agree with the possibility but still considered it worthwhile following up the lead of the light blue Nissan. It may only have been a slender lead, but it was the only lead that could be followed up on. 'Check it out.' He commanded.

'There is one other thing, Sir.' Daye said, her voice soft with a tinge of unusual hardness. 'I went with John Conway to the victims flat last night. He confirmed the disappearance of the coin collection.'

'As expected,' James said in a matter-of-fact manner.

'Yes, Sir.' Daye continued, her voice now showing a slight trace of irritation at her superior officer's interruption. 'But a charm bracelet has also disappeared.' Daye referred to her notes. 'It's inscribed 'To My Beloved Cathy.' It's a reference to Jack Manning's wife. She died of cancer seven years ago.'

'Why take an inscribed charm bracelet?' James asked mystified. 'What's the point of that?'

'Don't know, Sir.' Daye said resignedly. 'It has little value except for sentiment. But it was kept in the display cabinet, and it is now missing.'

'And yet more valuable items were left behind?'

'Yes, Sir.'

The office door opened with a flourish as a police sergeant rushed in. He was stony faced as he handed a handwritten note to James. His only spoken words were 'This was a phone call for your attention.'

CHAPTER
FIVE

★ ★ ★ ★

Daye pulled onto the car park of the communal allotments at canal side. Only a handful of cars were parked there; winter was approaching after all so there was not so much work needed doing to the land as was the case during the preceding few months. As she drove the unmarked police car into an empty parking space Daye smiled smugly to herself. The car in the next space was a light blue Nissan; the dent in its passenger door looked like it had been hit by another vehicle; red, going off the traces of red paint smeared into the scratch marks. She looked at James. A slight smile betrayed him; he too had seen the Nissan.

The communal allotments looked nearly deserted. Only a handful of men could be seen, either talking or else working on their sheds. *Routine maintenance* thought Daye.

'Excuse me.' James called out to a nearby elderly man who was busy repainting the front door of his shed. The old man turned and looked at him. 'Which allotment belongs to Jimmy MacGregor?'

The old man pointed to a well maintained blue and white shed at the other end of the allotments. A young man was stood outside the front door; *doing something to the hinges* thought Daye. The young man stopped as he saw the two officers approach him. He stood there holding what looked like a screwdriver.

Neither officer walked quickly towards the shed. But the young man was clearly agitated by their presence. The screwdriver, which Daye noticed had a black handle, was being gripped by a firm fist which was beginning to turn white from the pressure.

He suddenly turned and ran. Daye threw her car keys to James as she ran after the young man.

A well-trimmed hedge, about six feet high, separated the allotments from the canal. The young man, who was of stocky build but very athletic, headed for a small gap at the base of the hedge. But Daye was also very fit and was slowly catching up with him.

James, on the other hand, had not followed the fleeing man. As Daye had begun chasing him, James had caught the thrown car keys and turned around and rushed back to the car. Daye knew where the young man was headed. The nearest route off the canal bank was the bridge next to the Navigation Inn, just half a mile east of the allotments. As the young man threw himself at the gap in the hedge, she saw with delight that he had turned towards the east and towards the bridge at the Navigation Inn. The young man was trapped.

Daye, however, continued the chase. With gritted teeth and a steady running rhythm learnt from her athletics coach in the days before she joined the force, she kept pace with the young man who was now just twenty paces in front of her. But he had no rhythm to the way he ran. His head was back; his arms were flailing around; and his legs were wobbling. Daye did not need to catch him; he was going to burn out soon. As the bridge at the Navigation Inn came into sight around the bend in the canal, the young man suddenly stopped; James was stood in front of him blocking his escape.

Daye seized his arm and turned him to face her.

'Why are you running from us, Benny?' she demanded to know, quickly seizing the black handled screwdriver and forcefully snatching it from his grasp.

Benny Gordon stood open mouthed, red in the face, and breathless as he faced his captor. He was unable to speak.

'Are you in a hurry to get somewhere, Benny?' James asked casually, after he had strolled from the bridge to meet up with the running man and his sergeant.

'I haven't done anything.' He suddenly blurted out.

'Of course, you haven't. Benny.' Daye said with heavy sarcasm. 'That's why you're running away from us.'

'How do you know my name?'

Neither officer answered. With an officer on either side of him holding his arms firmly, Benny Gordon was taken back to the allotment shed of Jimmy MacGregor.

Daye looked at him as she held onto his arm. Benny was no more than twenty years of age, very muscular and strong, with a square jaw line under a round, clean shaven face, his blonde hair cut very short, almost to a skinhead. But it was his blue eyes that intrigued her. They were wild and frightened; almost childlike. If it was not for his adult size, he could easily have been mistaken for a lost infant separated from his parents.

'What are you doing here?' James asked as they reached the door of the shed.

'The door's dropped a bit.' Benny replied, his voice innocent and pleading. 'I was just putting it straight.'

Daye looked at the tool kit on the floor. All the tools in the roll up kit had black handles and each one had its place, except two spaces were vacant. She looked at the screwdriver in her hand. *Well, this fills one of those spaces*, she thought with obvious conviction, *but what belongs in the other space?*

'What's missing, Benny?' she demanded, pointing accusingly at the tool kit.

Benny stood looking at the kit but did not answer.

'We already know that it's a hammer.' James said accusingly. 'We've got it down at the station. Not only has it got blood on it but a rather nice set of prints as well. What's the betting that they're your prints?'

'I want an attorney.' Benny demanded.

'You've been watching too many American crime shows on T.V.' James said sarcastically. 'You want a solicitor.'

'Do I get a phone call?'

'After you've been charged,' James replied firmly, pushing him towards the armchair inside the shed, the arms of which Benny had to grab hold of to prevent himself from falling headfirst into the soft fabric.

'Sit,' Ordered James in a strong authoritative manner.

Benny did as he was told.

Daye began to look around the shed. The phone message had said that evidence was to be found here. *What evidence?* She wondered. It did not take long to find it though. Daye recovered the blue velvet case from beneath its covering of a dirty mud splattered blanket. As she opened the case to reveal the gold and silver coins, she turned to face Benny

Gordon. He looked impassively at the coins as though they held little interest for him.

'What have you to say about this?' James asked, indicating the coin collection.

Benny looked at the opened case which Daye was holding. He then looked casually away again.

'It probably belongs to Jimmy.' He said in a matter-of-fact manner. 'He sometimes keeps things in here that he doesn't want his wife to see.'

Daye's nostrils flared in thought. This was not the reaction that she had expected. James decided to take him in for further questioning. As he was led away Benny Gordon confirmed that the light blue Nissan with the dented passenger door was indeed his. Daye took his car keys while James took Benny, and the coin collection, to the unmarked police car that was still at the bridge.

She closed the shed door behind her although the repair that Benny had started had not been completed. As she walked with a jaunty gait towards the car park her mind was thinking in earnest causing her nostrils to flare yet again. *Something was wrong here*, she thought desperately to herself, *but what is it?*

Daye was about to start the engine of the light blue Nissan when a thought hit her. *We've got the coin collection*, she thought eagerly to herself, *but where's the charm bracelet? Why was that taken?* She withdrew the key from the ignition. *Why take an inexpensive item like a charm bracelet? Particularly as it could be so easily identified.* She pulled the lever that opened the boot.

That was where she started the search. Daye was going to examine and inspect every nook and cranny in the light blue Nissan. That charm bracelet had to be somewhere. She found it under the passenger seat. As she looked at the rabbit's foot and the gold heart that hung from it, she was not convinced that it confirmed Benny's guilt. Why should she have found it at all in the light blue Nissan?

CHAPTER
SIX

'I have informed my client as to his rights.' The overly smartly dressed and portly solicitor said reluctantly, obviously annoyed that his client, Benny, was ignoring his advice. 'And he is prepared to co-operate fully with your investigation.'

Benny sat fidgeting and uneasy beside his solicitor. *That solicitor wants this over and done with as soon as possible,* thought Daye, who sat opposite him and beside her own superior officer, James

'Do you recognise this, Benny?' James began, showing Benny the black handled hammer now encased in a polythene bag.

Benny nodded.

'For the benefit of the tape,' Daye said, indicating the recorder that was set into the wall at the end of the plain table that separated the interviewee and his solicitor from the police officers. 'Please answer yes or no to the questions.'

'Yes', he mumbled faintly, adding quickly. 'It's mine.'

'This was found at the home of Jack Manning and has been confirmed as the weapon that he was assaulted and murdered with. Can you explain why your hammer was at his home?'

Benny did not answer immediately. He looked wildly about him as though looking for a way out of the police interview room, but, finding no exit except the door where a uniformed constable was standing, he suddenly stared wide eyed at Daye who was looking directly back into his blue eyes and was smiling an encouraging smile. Tears filled Benny's eyes as he forced an almost childlike and lip curling attempt at a smile back. He then turned to face James.

'I killed him.' He shouted, tears rolling uncontrollably down his face.

'I really must advise you...........' the solicitor began to say in earnest.

'I killed him.' Benny shouted at him and then turned to face Daye and in a voice both tearful and pleading he repeated his confession. 'I killed him.'

Benny went on to explain what had happened on that fateful Tuesday. He had gone to Jack Manning's flat arriving there at approximately 10-15 a.m.

'I only took the hammer with me to frighten him.' He said through his sobs. 'He was a bad man who needed to be taught a lesson, but I didn't mean to hurt him. It just happened.'

'How did it 'just happen', Benny?' Daye prompted.

'I just wanted to talk to him, but he wouldn't listen. He ordered me out of his flat and when I wouldn't leave, he pushed me. I pushed him back.' Benny paused for a second or two. 'And then I hit him with the hammer. And then I hit him again.......... and then again.'

Benny's voice tailed away as he recounted the incident.

'How was Jack Manning a bad man?'

'He just was.'

'That's no answer, Benny.' Daye chided him like a mother to a naughty son. 'How was he a bad man? Had he done something to you?'

Benny slowly shook his head.

'Please speak for the tape, Benny.'

'No.' he mumbled feebly. 'Not to me.'

'Then to whom, Benny?'

'Not to me.' Benny shouted angrily. 'That's all I'm saying. He was a bad man who deserved what he got.'

'How well did you know Jack Manning? Was he a friend of yours? Or a friend of a friend?'

'I didn't know him.' Benny replied pitifully. 'I only met him for the first-time last Tuesday.'

'But you knew of him?'

'He was a bad man.' Benny repeated himself forcefully. 'He got what he deserved.'

'If you were there to punish him,' Daye probed. 'Why take the coin collection and the bracelet?'

Benny looked directly into Daye's eyes.

'What coin collection and bracelet?'

Daye sat up with a start. She looked directly back into Benny's eyes. *My God*! She thought with astonishment, *he doesn't know about them*!!!

'They were found in your possession, Benny.' James said firmly, leaning forward slightly to intimidate the wide-eyed young man. 'The coin collection was found in the shed.' James then produced another polythene bag, this one containing the bracelet. 'And this one was found in your car.'

'I've not seen that before.' Benny blurted, pointing to the charm bracelet. 'And that coin collection must have been

Jimmy's. I told you; he keeps things there that he doesn't want his wife to see.'

'The coin collection belongs to Jack Manning.' James said coldly, with a menacing hint of annoyance. 'And so does this bracelet that was found under the passenger seat of your car. How did it get there, Benny, if you didn't put it there?'

'I don't know.' he stammered and flustered, waving his arms wildly as though trying to reinforce his words. 'Honest. I don't know.'

Daye watched Benny intently. Why was he confessing to murder but not theft? And yet she believed him. But if Benny had not taken those items, then who had?

James continued to ask probing questions about the coin collection and the charm bracelet, but Benny's answers remained steadfastly the same. He was denying all knowledge of them.

'Why did you return to Jack Manning's flat in the afternoon?' Daye suddenly asked, noticing out of the corner of her eye that even James was taken by surprise by her question.

Benny shrugged his shoulders.

'I didn't.' He said with utmost surprise in his voice. 'I went home and stayed there. I didn't go anywhere.'

'You parked your car on the library car park, didn't you?'

'Yes.' Benny readily confirmed. 'It was the nearest parking space that I could find to the flat.'

'But your car was parked there again in the afternoon.'

'I didn't go out in the afternoon.'

'So how was your car able to return to that car park?'

Benny averted his eyes from Daye's stare.

'I didn't go out in the afternoon.' He repeated.

He's lying, Daye thought firmly to herself. *Oh yes, he may not have returned to the car park himself, but his car had.* The manageress had stated that the light blue Nissan had been on the car park twice on that day. *So, who had been driving it?*

'Did you lend your car to somebody, Benny? A friend perhaps?'

Benny bit his lip as he bent his head forward. Daye repeated her question. Benny refused to answer except to say that he had not gone back to the car park.

What is he playing at? The words whirled around Daye's mind. Here was Benny readily confessing to murder, and yet he was denying all knowledge of the theft or offering any explanation as to how his car had returned to the library car park that Tuesday afternoon. Was he hiding something? Daye was convinced that he was.

James continued to probe about the car; Benny continued to say that he had not been out that afternoon and refused to say where his car had been. But the more serious offence had been the murder and Benny was prepared to make a statement confessing to the crime. James settled for that.

Once Daye had taken Benny's statement and he had signed it, she handed him over to the custody sergeant who led him away to the cells. But that was not the end of it as far as Daye was concerned. As she made her way back to the office, she went back over all the evidence in her mind trying to analyse and reanalyse all the information. The case was a jigsaw puzzle with too many key pieces missing.

James was sat behind his desk again as Daye entered the office.

'I want to make this our top priority.' He said firmly, pointing to the file in front of him. It was the file of the six attacks on those women with young daughters. 'He's been away for four years.........'

'We haven't finished with the murder of Jack Manning, Sir.' She interrupted forcefully, closing the office door behind her and heading towards the coffee machine where she turned to face her superior officer. 'We've got the confession of a young man who had never met Jack before. Yet he goes to his flat and bludgeons him to death without any apparent motive other than saying that Jack was a bad man who deserved to be punished. Punished for what?'

'It's not a false confession.' James said slowly, leaning back in his chair. 'The hammer belonged to him; the blood-stained fingerprints on it are his as are the prints in the flat. And his description of the way he murdered the victim tallies exactly with what happened. Property belonging to the victim has also been found in his possession, incidentally by you.'

'And then we have his confession.' Daye added venomously.

'You're not going to say he is innocent, are you?'

'Somebody stole those items out of Jack's flat. And I don't think for one minute it was that poor sod that we've got locked up in the cells.'

'So, who took them?' James asked solemnly. 'And why?'

'As to whom I don't know.' Daye conceded but added with a fierce certainty. 'But they were taken and planted to guarantee a murder conviction against Benny Gordon.'

'Don't you think that's a bit fanciful?' James challenged. 'Benny Gordon committed the murder of Jack Manning. You're ignoring the evidence.'

'It may very well have been Benny.'

'Then what are we arguing about?'

'Motive,' Daye answered defiantly. 'Somebody put Benny up to it. He didn't just pick Jack's name out of a hat and then bludgeoned him to death. Benny Gordon committed that murder on behalf of somebody else and that person is just as guilty of the crime as he is.'

James did not answer. He sat looking thoughtful in his chair as though pondering the possibility.

'Have you got someone in mind?' He said eventually.

'Have you got last night's paper, Sir?'

James rummaged through the paperwork on his desk until he found last night's copy of the 'Bellingham Advertiser'. He handed it to Daye.

'Look at this.' She said triumphantly, showing James the headline on the front page; 'Brutal Murder of Local Man.' 'it says here that a man was found murdered, name not given. It also doesn't mention anything about any items being stolen. And it only says that the police are investigating. It doesn't mention any officers' names.'

'What's your point?' James asked, obviously intrigued.

'That message that sent us to the allotments.' Daye said firmly.' It mentioned the victim's name; it mentioned that evidence would be found; and, more importantly, the message was for your attention. How had the caller known all that?'

James took the paper back off Daye and read the article. He had obviously read it before but not this intently.

'That is one person I would definitely like to interview.' Daye concluded, her voice as hard as iron. James nodded his head in agreement.

CHAPTER
SEVEN

Anne-Marie De Wynter did not suit black, but as she stood beside the entrance of the crematorium she felt as black as her clothes. This was the part of her plan that she did not relish but was compelled to go through with. She had loved her Uncle Jack once; even still had feelings for him like the schoolgirl crush that she had once when she was thirteen. But it had not been a love that Uncle Jack had reciprocated. On the contrary, Jack Manning had told her not to be silly and to behave herself. He was not, nor ever done, going to take advantage of her. In a way Anne-Marie respected him for it, but she would not forgive him for rejecting her. And as she mingled with the other mourners, mainly relatives of Jack Manning, as they waited for the hearse to arrive, Anne-Marie forced the tears to roll down her face. It would have been expected of her anyway. Pat Conway, held firmly by her husband John, held Anne-Marie's hand tightly, and smiled kindly at her through reddened and tear-stained eyes. They walked into the crematorium together, hand in hand, behind Jack's coffin.

The service in the Chapel of the crematorium was simple and short; Jack had not been a very religious person and had very rarely attended church. That had been the reason for a no Church funeral, and only a committal service at the crematorium. But as the service ended and the curtains encircled the brass handled coffin, a lump of emotion arose in Anne-Marie's throat. She still loved her Uncle Jack; and yet she felt no regrets over what had happened on that Tuesday morning.

Light rain began to fall as the mourners filed silently out of the Chapel. Very few words were exchanged between them, and Anne-Marie could only see looks of stunned shock on their faces. No one mentioned the name 'Benny Gordon' although everyone there had heard it; had heard it and hated it.

Pat asked Anne-Marie to return with them to their home for some lunch. She declined the invitation.

'I'd like too.' She tried to explain, her voice heavy with emotion. 'But I would prefer to be on my own this afternoon.'

Pat nodded her understanding.

But Anne-Marie would not be alone that afternoon. With a cursory glance towards the car park next to the Chapel of Remembrance, Anne-Marie saw a dark blue Rover with its driver sitting impatiently waiting for her. She kissed Pat and John goodbye, more tears streaming down her face, before she turned and headed for the car park. The car's engine gave out a deep throated roar as it came into life well before Anne-Marie was in shouting distance of the little brick-built Chapel.

The drive to the 'Red Hills' was silent and lasted for about twenty minutes. As the car drove into the country park fresh black clouds appeared overhead and unleashed such a fierce downpour that the driver had to speed up his windscreen wipers to maximum to cope with the rainwater. Fortunately, the picnic area deep within the park was, not surprisingly, empty of all signs of life. As the car came to a halt on the reddish coloured gravel that served as the car park, Anne-Marie looked around the picnic area. Elm, ash, and oak trees surrounded it making it appear that only she and the driver were the only people on the planet, a perfect place for a quiet chat.

'How was your holiday?' Anne-Marie asked, looking at the sun-tanned driver beside her. 'You look well.'

'I'm not here to talk about holidays.' The driver snapped back at her, his rough hands fidgeting uncontrollably on the steering wheel. 'What the hell happened?'

Anne-Marie smiled smugly. She partially lowered the window to allow some of the damp cooling air to enter the car. It refreshed her.

'How did you find out?' She asked casually, turning to face the nervous, well-built man with the angled and chiselled features. Anne-Marie knew him to be thirty-seven years of age, yet his weather-beaten face made him look so much older.

'I got back from Tunisia yesterday.' He replied sombrely, his eyes wandering in all directions except towards Anne-Marie. 'I rang up Benny last night to see how he had got on at the allotments. I'd asked him to do some work for me, you see, while I was away. He wasn't in so I phoned his mother. She told me what had happened. I couldn't believe it. I thought at first that it was a sick Joke.'

'Some sick joke!' Anne-Marie interrupted angrily. 'Jack was my uncle.'

'I know, I know.' He agreed apologetically. 'But could Benny kill someone? I just couldn't take it in. She then asked me had I ever heard of Jack Manning. Apparently, no one in the Gordon family knew of anyone by that name.'

'What did you say, Jimmy?' Anne-Marie prompted, probing for a weakness.

'I said that I had never heard of him either.' Jimmy replied sheepishly, adding quickly. 'Well, I had never met him. And it was only after the phone conversation had ended that I eventually remembered that he was your uncle. But how had Benny known him?'

'Well, he was your friend and not mine,' Anne-Marie said, the accusation in her voice crystal clear. 'How had he known of my uncle?'

Jimmy turned to face Anne-Marie, the look of wild shock on his face clearly visible to her.

It was a gentle accusation, but an accusation, nevertheless. Anne-Marie was the personal assistant to the managing director of Ashcroft's Fabrications; Jimmy MacGregor was the foreman of the detail production shop. They had become friends ever since Anne-Marie had begun work there three years before, and then had become more than friends when Jimmy's marriage to Susan had hit the rocks during the summer of the previous year. They had met in secret usually at the allotment shed because Jimmy had been afraid of possible repercussions should his wife ever become aware, or suspicious, of their affair. It was not so much the fear of his wife that Jimmy was afraid of, it was more what he stood to lose; her father was none other than Anne-Marie's boss, the managing director of Ashcroft's Fabrications. He could lose his home, job, just about everything. That was why he had ended his relationship with Anne-Marie to save his marriage. The holiday in Tunisia had been part of the reconciliation process.

But Anne-Marie's accusation did not involve Susan, although deep down she did not like having to take second place to another woman. Her accusation had involved his friendship with Benny Gordon, the killer of her beloved Uncle Jack. All Jimmy had done was to befriend the lonely, shy, and introverted Benny. He had first met him as he had wandered aimlessly around the allotments, 'just looking', he would say if anyone spoke to him, 'just looking.' Slowly but surely, Jimmy had managed to strike up a bit of a conversation with Benny, although to get any information out of him was like pulling teeth, painstaking to say the least. But Benny had proved to be a good worker and seemed to enjoy helping on the allotment. And so, he came every weekend, and sometimes during the week as well, turning the allotment shed into almost a second home for him. He had frequently been present when Anne-Marie had been there.

'What are you accusing me of?' Jimmy demanded to know, his voice high pitched and incredulous. 'I've been in Tunisia for the past fortnight. What the hell could I have to do with anything?'

'As far as I know,' Anne-Marie began to explain, 'Benny has never even spoken to my Uncle Jack, let alone known where he lived. Indeed, I've never so much as mentioned his name to him or spoken to him about my uncle. I've only spoken of my uncle to you.' adding ominously, 'and spoken to you about his love of chess and coins. Coins that were found in your allotment shed.'

'What?' Jimmy screamed. 'You mean his coin collection...............?'

'Found in your shed.' Anne-Marie repeated quietly. 'Why had Benny hidden them there do you think?'

Jimmy threw his head back into the headrest of his seat. His face was a picture of despair and fear.

'O Jesus.' He suddenly swore angrily. 'I didn't know about that.'

'Do you think the police would believe you?'

'Hey!' He exclaimed in defiance. 'Leave me out of this.'

'The police will want to know how someone who hadn't known anything about Jack had got hold of the information regarding his valuable coin collection.' Anne-Marie persisted, her voice as strong and firm as iron. 'That information could only have come from you.'

Despite his rich suntan Anne-Marie could see the blood slowly draining away from Jimmy's face. *He's frightened now* she thought gleefully to herself, *how's he going to get himself out of this?*

'I swear to you,' Jimmy pleaded pitifully, his blue eyes betraying his fear and dread. 'I did not speak to Benny about your Uncle Jack. I don't know where he got the information from.'

'Don't worry, Jimmy.' Anne-Marie said softly, reaching her hand across to slowly stroke his thinning black hair. 'I know you were not involved. But would the police see it that way?'

Jimmy slowly shook his head.

'I don't know what to think.' He said eventually, 'He must have spoken to someone else about your uncle. That is the only way that he could have found out about your uncle and his coin collection.'

'Yes.' Anne-Marie agreed, adding with carefully worded gravity, 'but the police would want to know who. What name would you give them?'

Jimmy suddenly flung open the car door and walked, hands in pockets, through the pouring rain towards one of the picnic tables. Anne-Marie watched him, inwardly smiling to herself, and thinking that *this loose end was going to be nicely tied up and finished with.*

She decided to join Jimmy at the picnic table.

The rain was becoming lighter now, but the wind was getting up causing the tops of the nearby trees to sway. With one hand holding her black hat, with the gold stitching around the edge, in place whilst the other held her black leather coat clasped tightly about her, she skipped lightly through the rain filled puddles on the gravel car park towards Jimmy who had now sat down on one of the wooden benches beside a table. His dark blue slacks and thin woollen jacket, presumably his travel attire from Tunisia, were soon soaked and sodden. Yet, as Anne-Marie approached him, she noticed that he did not seem to realise. His face was tilted to the still falling rain and his expression was one of abject misery and deep thought.

Good, Anne-Marie thought callously to herself, *he doesn't know what to do.*

'Your world isn't going to fall apart you know.' She said reassuringly.

'Isn't it?' Jimmy replied despondently. 'If this ever got out to my wife that I was the link between Benny Gordon and Jack Manning, what do you think her first question will be? It will be 'How the hell did you know of Jack Manning?' And how do I answer that? Through having an affair with his niece. That would go down like a lead brick and my feet wouldn't touch the ground as we flew through the divorce court.'

'Why does she need to know?'

Jimmy slowly turned his head towards Anne-Marie. He looked quizzically at her.

'You've got a lot to lose if our relationship should ever become public knowledge.' Anne-Marie said coldly, adding with menace. 'But so have I.'

'What have you got to lose?'

'People are asking, as are the police, 'how did Benny know Jack?" Anne-Marie replied, 'especially Jack's relatives. How do you think they would react to me if they knew that Benny was a friend of a man that I was having an affair with? I don't think that they would take too kindly to that do you? I could be accused of giving you the information about Jack so that you, in turn, could give it to Benny.'

'So, what do we do?'

'There is not, nor ever been, any sort of relationship between us.' Anne-Marie's voice was quiet but full of authority. It was an order. 'We never met at the allotment shed or anywhere else for that matter. Do you understand?'

Jimmy nodded slowly. He understood.

'But what do we do about Benny?' He suddenly asked, a note of anxiety creeping into his voice. 'He knows about us.'

'He hasn't spoken about us yet, has he?' Anne-Marie said confidently. 'And why should he?'

A faint smile slowly crossed Jimmy's face.

Good, thought Anne-Marie with contempt. *He'll do as he is told; and now to make sure.*

The rain was beginning to fall heavily again as she stood in front of Jimmy. No words were spoken as she opened her coat to reveal the black knee length dress that she wore underneath. Jimmy was mesmerised as he watched her, oblivious to the rain that was soaking both. He caught her coat as she threw it at him. He threw it onto the sodden surface of the wooden table, but he did not see exactly where as his eyes stared with a rigid fixation on Anne-Marie and what she was doing.

To Jimmy, Anne-Marie was doing a very seductive striptease in the rain. She was taking off her clothes one by one and throwing them to him. He, in turn, was blindly throwing them onto her black coat although he could not be certain exactly where they were landing; his eyes never leaving the slowly revealing form of Anne-Marie.

But Anne-Marie was doing more than a striptease for her former lover. She was dominating and controlling him, only he did not realise it. Before this afternoon was over, Jimmy would be fully under her control, totally unable to reveal anything of their relationship to anyone, certainly not to Susan, and especially not to the police. Jimmy had a lot to lose; Anne-Marie had everything to gain.

Her dress, hat, slip, shoes and tights slowly followed the coat onto the picnic table. As she stood before him wearing only a smile and a pair of shiny, black, rain soaked, knickers, Anne-Marie looked coldly at Jimmy. His eyes were transfixed by her proud breasts, firmly pointing towards him, raindrops falling like tears from her nipples. The rain which washed over her body made Anne-Marie feel sensual and alive, but she was not doing this strip for pleasure although she was finding it enjoyable. She had done her strip perfectly; Jimmy was hooked.

With a smile of deep satisfaction, she removed her last garment, the soaking wet knickers. She threw them at Jimmy's hypnotised and overcome face with its hanging jaw line. He caught the satin underwear in his teeth before throwing them quickly onto the other clothes.

She was naked; he was dressed. But she was in control; he was the slave.

Slowly, her body, slippery from the rain, and her long blond hair flattened against her head and shoulders, she approached her victim. He did nothing to stop her sitting astride his legs facing him; or to stop her from kissing him, allowing her tongue to invade his mouth. Nor did he complain when her hand moved towards his groin.

Anne-Marie did not know as to how long they had made love on that rain-soaked bench while more rain lashed down onto them. She wanted Jimmy's silence and now she had it, but she was going to enjoy the experience anyway, and why not? This may have been the day of Jack's funeral, but he was hardly able to claim that what she was doing was in bad taste was he? No one was in any position to complain, except, of course, for the person with the prying eyes watching from behind the protective screen of the nearby trees.

CHAPTER
EIGHT

The funeral ceremony had not gone the way that Anne-Marie had thought it had. She may have loved to have been the person in control, but on this occasion she had not; only she had not realised it. And that was because there had been someone at the funeral that Anne-Marie had been totally unaware of. She would no doubt have behaved differently if she had known that this person had been present, so perhaps the funeral needs to be revisited.

The book of remembrance lay opened on the page displaying the names of all the people that had died on that date over the past thirty years. They had been either cremated or buried in the extensive cemetery that surrounded the crematorium and the little brick-built Chapel of Remembrance, but this elaborately designed book made sure that they were never forgotten.

Jessica Morris stood in the entrance to the Chapel and watched the mourners gather for Jack Manning's funeral. She did not really know why she was there; she would certainly not be made welcome amongst the group of sombre people dressed all in black that were only about fifty yards from her. It was not that Jessica was a bad person or anything like that; most people would have described her as pleasant and charming. She was a young woman of twenty-four, slim, dark haired with a ready smile that could put anyone immediately at their ease. Dressed conservatively in a dark trouser suit under her full length dark grey coat, she was visually acceptable for the occasion.

But Jack Manning's relatives would have disliked her by association. She had come in the hope of talking to one, or possibly, two, of them; perhaps even to learn something that could help her cousin. But then again, why should any relative of Jack Manning help the cousin of Benny Gordon?

I should have known that this would've been a bad idea, she complained to herself bitterly. *This is a day for Jack's family to grieve; hardly a time to be forgiving of his murderer.*

But why had Benny committed such a terrible crime? That had not made any sense to either her or to Aunt Julie, Benny's mother. At first both Aunt Julie and she had thought that the police had made a horrendous mistake and that Benny would be released soon. But as they were told of the evidence, and especially of Benny's confession, both Jessica and her aunt had gone into a state of shock. This had been too unbelievable to be true, and yet it had been the truth. And even a court of law had believed the evidence to be true as it remanded him in custody to await his trial. *Why had you done it, Benny?* Jessica had repeated that question to herself hundreds, if not thousands, of times. But there was never any answer. No one, not even the police, had been able to answer the question of 'why?' It became an even deeper mystery when it became apparent to everyone that Benny had no connection with the victim either. So why kill him?

Jessica hoped to find some answers amongst the relatives of Jack Manning. But this really was a bad idea of hers.

Now was not the time to remind them of the name 'Benny Gordon.' Jessica decided to return home to be with her aunt; that was where she was needed now.

As she took one last look at the mourners, Jessica said a silent prayer for them. She loved her young cousin dearly; he was almost a little brother for her, but she could understand the feelings of Jack Manning's relatives. *God bless you all*, she said to herself, *we all deserve to know the truth.*

Who's that? Jessica suddenly asked herself as she strained her eyes to look through the drizzle at the three people walking behind the coffin as it was taken into the crematorium. *I recognise John Conway; he's been almost a family spokesman since the murder occurred. The woman he is holding must be his wife I assume. But who is the young woman with them? She looks familiar. My God it is! What's that bitch doing here?*

Jessica's mouth fell open.

She strained her eyes to get the clearest view possible. *Yes*, she said to herself with absolute certainty; *that's Ann Walker*!! Questions suddenly flooded into the Mind of Jessica Morris; *what's that scheming whore been up to now? What's her connection with Jack Manning? She must be close to him because she is leading the mourners into the crematorium. Was she involved in his death? Oh my God did she know Benny? He wouldn't have stood a chance with her.*

Jessica bit her lip as the mourners slowly disappeared into the crematorium. She turned back into the Chapel of Remembrance, her hands to her face as she sank deep into thought. She had not seen Ann Walker since the days of her youth spent in the learning halls of Red Hills High School, set beside the country park named for the red sandy coloured soil that covered the area. She had been in the same class as Ann Walker and knew well of her reputation; a reputation that had been well deserved. But her activities had been difficult to prove. Ann Walker had been very devious.

Names immediately came to mind; names such as Phil Green, Joshua Anderson, and Frank Dawes, to name only three. There had been others of course, boys who had behaved out of character and had done something that they had later regretted. Those boys had been caught and punished; others had escaped punishment. But behind them all had been one girl lurking in the shadows, Ann Walker.

Jessica had thought like the other girls and had initially cheered Ann Walker on. Why were the boys so stupid as to allow themselves to be used like that? They were being made to look foolish; a mere girl having a lark with them, playing a joke on them. This was girl power at its best, putting the boys in their place.

But the joke stopped with Joshua Anderson. Jessica remembered him as a sensitive boy who only wanted to become a doctor. His grades were good in school, not excitingly good, but good enough to start him on a hoped-for medical career. Jessica had liked him, not as a potential boyfriend of course, but had liked him as a person who was kind and gentle; he was going to make a superb doctor. *Why did he steal that money?*

Jessica and a few other girls as well, were shocked when it was revealed that the France trip money had been stolen by Joshua. No one regarded him as a thief, but the money had never been recovered. What had happened to it? Rumours amongst the girls was rife. They all pointed their fingers at Ann Walker, although no one could provide any proof. They just seemed to know that it was her. Jessica had shared that view; a view that was not to change as other boys stepped inexplicably outside of their characters. And each time the finger of suspicion amongst the girls always pointed to Ann Walker as someone who had something to do with it. The boys never blamed Ann, maybe they were too embarrassed to admit that a mere slip of a girl had made fools of them, and yet something, or someone, had made them do things that they would not have normally done. But whoever had been responsible had never been caught, but a burning question always remained; why was Ann Walker always associated with those same boys just before they did whatever each one had later come to regret?

And now innocent cousin Benny had done something that was out of character for him. Was it a coincidence? Could it really have been just chance that both Benny and Ann just happened to have known the murder victim Jack Manning? Or had Benny just become the latest victim of the 'Praying Mantis,' the nickname that the girls of Red Hills High School had given to a predator who lured and preyed on defenceless members of the male species, Ann Walker.

And 'Praying Mantis' was an ideal nickname for Ann Walker. The 'Praying Mantis' would lie perfectly still and lure its victims to come close to her when she would suddenly pounce and devour her victim. The only difference with Ann Walker was that after luring boys to her she used her womanly wiles to get what she wanted.

Jessica ran those questions over and over in her mind. She was still thinking them as she stepped out of the Chapel of Remembrance just as a dark blue Rover drove onto the small car park and pulled up within a few feet of where she was standing. Jessica looked at the driver for a moment. He was sun-tanned and very nervous; Jessica looked at his hands as they fidgeted and drummed repeatedly on the steering wheel. But her eyes then settled on his sharp features. *I know him from somewhere*, she thought distractedly, assuming that he must relate to Jack Manning's funeral although he did not leave his car to join the other mourners who had already entered the crematorium.

That's Jimmy MacGregor!!! Jessica suddenly realised although she had only seen him a couple of times with her cousin Benny. *What's he doing here*? She thought inquisitively, *and why is he looking so nervous?*

Jessica took one step backwards into the doorway of the Chapel of Remembrance. It seemed a prudent thing to do while she tried to understand what was happening at this funeral. After all, Jimmy had told her aunt last night that he had never heard of Jack Manning and yet here he was. Granted he was not actually attending the ceremony itself but, even so, why was he sitting in his car watching the entrance to the crematorium?

Jessica soon got her answer. From her concealed position within the Chapel of Remembrance, Jessica could see both Jimmy MacGregor and the entrance to the crematorium. She watched carefully as the mourners slowly began to leave, each one taking the time to shake the hand of the vicar who had performed the ceremony. Then out came John Conway and his wife with Ann Walker. They too shook the vicar's hand before standing outside the Crematorium entrance in the light drizzle. Jessica obviously could not hear what was being said but it was a short conversation followed by a kiss to both Conway's' from Ann. She then turned and headed towards the Chapel of Remembrance.

Jessica stood further back into the Chapel of Remembrance; she did not want to be seen by Ann until she had figured out more of what was happening here. The Rover's engine suddenly gave out a deep throated roar; Jessica stared out the door to see why. Ann was heading straight for the Rover where the nervous Jimmy MacGregor was showing signs of growing impatience.

She's not going to get into the car, is she? Thought Jessica incredulously, watching as Ann approached the Rover and then climbed swiftly into the passenger seat. *My God!! She is.*

Jessica's mouth involuntarily dropped open as Jimmy MacGregor sped away. Almost without thinking, Jessica ran to her own car that was parked nearby. She nearly wrenched the door off its hinges in her hurry to get inside. She did not even wait to buckle up her seat belt as she switched on the engine and sped after the dark blue Rover.

Through the cemetery and out onto the main road raced Jimmy MacGregor's Rover with Jessica's less powerful white Toyota trying desperately to keep up. *He's in a hurry wherever he is going*, thought Jessica, trying to control the car whilst struggling to put on her seat belt. Eventually she was safely buckled in, but MacGregor's car was in the distance and pulling away from her. He was not heading toward town, but rather more to the East as though heading for the Red Hills district, a sort of self-contained village within the town's borough. It was an area that Jessica knew well having spent most of her early life there and had attended the local high school. But as she turned into Dorchester

Drive, the long tree lined avenue that served as the Red Hills main through road, her heart sank; she had lost the dark blue Rover.

Where the hell could they have been going to? Jessica desperately thought to herself as she looked keenly down every side road that she slowly passed. *Why come to the Red Hills? Ann had left this area soon after leaving the school. And MacGregor did not live around here either.*

Jessica racked her brain for an answer but came up with nothing. But as she left the centre of Red Hills behind her with its shops and countless back streets, Jessica found herself approaching the residential part of the area with new, and not so new, housing estates on the left opposite the country park. It was at the end of Dorchester Drive, on the far side of the park, that Red Hills High School was to be found. Jessica stopped the car.

Surely, she has not gone back to school, a bemused Jessica thought. *What would be the point of that? Besides it is a school day. There would be several hundred children there plus the teachers.*

Jessica turned to look towards the park. The rain was coming down heavier now, the park would be empty of people; but Ann knew that park well. *Yes*, Jessica thought with a smile, *Ann knew that park well. That's where she has gone, but where exactly?*

Every child that attended Red Hills High School knew that park; from biology classes looking for fauna and flora, to cross country running, the pupils of the school had made good use of that park. It had three entrances; the main entrance, which was just off Dorchester Drive, that lead to the running track and then to the picnic area beyond;

the second entrance was by the school gates which lead to a small car park next to the old farmhouse that had been turned into a museum. A track from the farmhouse also lead to the picnic area. The third entrance was on the far side of the park and was mainly used by the park rangers and gardeners employed by the council. It was a rough track which led through the trees behind the school and emerged at the small car park next to the farmhouse.

I'll bet money she has gone to the picnic area, Jessica thought with a smile, *it is nice and secluded there.*

Jessica slowly pulled away from the kerb and headed for the entrance to the park. At the last second, she decided, however, not to use the main entrance but rather the entrance at the school gates. She could park at the farmhouse and walk up to the picnic area.

The car park was just as she remembered it. The red gravel was uneven and full of puddles but otherwise tidy and well looked after. She could barely see the school though because the trees that she remembered were now very tall and thick although most had lost their canopy of leaves. As expected, the car park was empty; the museum being closed for the winter months. Jessica parked her car and walked across to the other side of the car park.

The car park had two entrances, but neither exited to the same place. The entrance that Jessica had used led only back to the school gates, whilst the other led to a fork; the right fork leading to the picnic area whilst the left led to the trees behind the school and therefore ultimately to the entrance at the far side of the park.

Jessica took the right fork and prayed to herself that her assumption of Ann was correct. Not that she was afraid of failure, it was just that the wind and rain was getting heavy again and she did not want to catch a chill.

As she walked through the trees, she could make out the outline of a single vehicle parked in the picnic area. Jessica smiled to herself; the vehicle was a dark blue Rover. Stealthily she took to the trees and progressed with caution towards the car park and the picnic tables. She suddenly stopped, her eyes wide open, when she saw that Jimmy MacGregor and Anne Walker were at one of the picnic tables. It was not so much that Jimmy was sat down and that his clothes were thoroughly drenched; it was the fact that Ann was standing in front of him completely naked.

What happened next led Jessica to believe that what she was seeing was not real, but rather surreal. She watched transfixed as Ann sat on Jimmy's knee and then proceeded to make love to him. The rain was lashing down and yet neither one of them seemed to care as they embraced, kissed, and fondled each other with wild abandon. They were in a world of their own, a world of ecstasy, and they obviously did not care who knew it.

Jessica had not known what to expect when she had first set off in pursuit of the dark blue Rover. She had thought that maybe she would have caught them plotting, or perhaps even meeting up with someone else, maybe another conspirator. But this had never even crossed her mind. She would have been hard pressed to believe that MacGregor and Ann were friends but making love in the rain went far beyond friendship. It also went far beyond the bounds of possibility that Jimmy MacGregor's claims that he had never heard of Jack Manning were other than complete lies. And if he had lied, which Jessica was now convinced that he had, then the person that he was now copulating with would have been his more than capable tutor.

Jessica turned away from them and began to make her way back to her car. Different thoughts and theories began to fill her mind. She could not make sense of it all yet, but one thing was evidently clear; poor Benny had fallen victim to the 'lure of the Praying Mantis'.

CHAPTER
NINE

★ ★ ★ ★

The little girl was rigid with the fear and horror of the situation. The knife felt cold and sharp against the soft skin of her throat, but her tears felt hot as they rolled uncontrollably down her pink cheeks. Her mother, shaking with dread and begging for her daughter's life, was almost ripping her own clothes off in response to the man's commands.

He was short, about five foot three or four, wearing a dark blue track suit and a matching balaclava, and was holding a fierce-some eight-inch blade to her six-year-old daughter's throat. But it was his eyes that frightened the mother the most, they were blue, piercing, and wide, and showed angry through the slits of the balaclava. He was a man that needed to be obeyed.

'Hurry up, Bitch.' He ordered, his voice deep and yet effeminate.

The mother, hurrying to obey the man's orders, fumbled and struggled to remove her underwear, her fingers tripping over each other in their anxiety to please the man. She eventually removed the last of her torn clothing and threw them onto the ground beside her green Range Rover, the vehicle in which she had driven to this place.

A sudden growl and the high-pitched scream of the man momentarily disoriented the mother. She looked with horror as her daughter fell forward, blood streaming from a knife wound to the throat, while the man struggled and slashed at the attentions of a growling and biting German shepherd dog.

An elderly man, walking stick raised defiantly and with an angry look on his face, came from out of the trees and advanced menacingly towards the knife welding maniac. But the mother's concern was for her daughter. She rushed forward and grabbed her child, pulling her away from the man whilst, at the same time trying to staunch the wound with the remnants of her slip.

Her assailant did not try to stop her, nor try to recapture her child. His hands were full of a snarling adult male German shepherd that had gripped his right arm and was trying to wrestle him to the ground. It was strong and soon had the man writhing in the dirt, whimpering and pleading with the old man to call the dog off. The old man stood steadfast and strong but whistled to his dog anyway. It heeded the sound and rushed to the side of his master.

But the old man had fallen for a ploy. The balaclava wearing man, his track suit torn and dirty, suddenly leapt nimbly for the driver's door of the green Range Rover which he forcibly yanked open. The old man shouted, and the dog leapt forward but the knifeman had thrown himself into the vehicle and, with a vicious kick at the dog's head, slammed the door shut again before the angry beast could get at him.

As the old man advanced to help his dog, the Range Rover's engine sprang into life. With spinning wheels that churned up the gravel track the green vehicle lurched forward and headed speedily away through the trees.

The naked woman then praised God and comforted her frightened daughter as the old man took out his mobile phone and dialled 999.

D.S. Daye Durham poured herself yet another cup of coffee and then turned to face her superior officer who was behind his desk reading yet another report. He shook his head when she offered to pour him a drink.

'The answers are always the same,' She began resignedly, moving to take her place behind her own desk which was next to D.I. Buchan's. 'Benny Gordon is regarded as polite, friendly if somewhat shy, quiet almost to the point of monastic silence, but always willing to help anybody; hardly the profile of a homicidal maniac.'

'But he did attack Jack Manning.' James reminded her.

'I know.' She conceded. 'But I'm still convinced someone else was behind him.'

'Based on what?'

'One of his neighbours is a Mrs. Kennedy.' Daye began earnestly, looking directly towards James. 'Her day off is a Tuesday and she is prepared to swear that on the Tuesday of Jack Manning's death she saw Benny Gordon at his front door during the afternoon. He was dealing with some door-to-door salesman.'

'What time was this?'

'Sometime between 3 and 4,' Daye answered quickly, adding, 'Mrs. Kennedy also noticed that Benny's car wasn't parked outside.'

'So, he had lent it to someone.'

'Yes. Unfortunately, Mrs. Kennedy couldn't say who to.' But then added thoughtfully, 'But she has noticed that a young woman, tall, blonde, probably early twenties, has been calling on him recently.'

'Could it be a girlfriend maybe?'

'According to his mother, and Cousin Jessica, he doesn't, nor has ever, had a girlfriend.'

'Then who is she?'

'The neighbours don't know,' Daye rummaged through the papers on her desk and withdrew a brown manila folder from the pile. She handed it to James 'The lab boys washed that 999 tape through the computer. Despite the disguise that she tried, they think that the voice belonged to a young woman and that she was certainly not Irish.'

James flicked through the pages that lay within the folder.

'What about the phone number?' James suddenly asked. 'Who owned the phone?'

'It was a mobile phone, sir.' Daye replied quietly, but added ominously, 'and bought by someone who doesn't exist and lives in a house that hasn't been built.'

'Can they trace where the call was made from?' James asked hopefully.

'From somewhere in Bellingham.' Daye looked downhearted as she spoke. 'This girl has covered her tracks well.'

'Interesting, isn't it?' Was all James remarked, but after a short pause, he added, 'We need to find and talk to that woman.'

'You think that this mysterious girlfriend and the anonymous phone caller are one and the same?'

James did not answer but shook his shoulders as though it was a possibility but could not prove it.

'I think you are on to something.' James said, his words sounding encouraging to Daye. 'See what else you can find out about her. I'm having no joy with Jack Manning. I just cannot find anything remotely damaging about him. As well as coin collecting his main hobby appears to be playing and coaching chess. He goes into schools sometimes giving coaching lessons to the chess clubs.'

'Is he ever alone with the kids?'

'No.' James said firmly. 'At least one teacher is always with the kids.'

'Are there any problems at all?'

'Not one apparently,' James answered firmly and with conviction. 'If Benny Gordon is convinced that Jack Manning is a bad man who deserved to be punished, then I have yet to find out what he is a bad man for doing.'

The office door suddenly opened. It was a uniformed sergeant.

'He's struck again, Sir.' He said gravely, 'at the Red Hills Country Park.'

James and Daye jumped to their feet and raced for the door. Shouting orders as he went, James followed Daye down the steps to the car park and leapt into the passenger seat of the unmarked police car. Daye, her heart beating with anticipation, turned on the ignition and revved the engine.

Red Hills was more than a twenty-minute drive from Templegate, even in a racing police car with its siren screaming. Daye concentrated on the road whilst her superior spoke animatedly over the radio, receiving information and then issuing orders accordingly.

'Get that description of the car and its registration number out to all units. 'He barked, adding with gusto. 'And get that bloody bird in the air, there's a lot of back streets in Red Hills. I don't want to lose him just because he might be hiding up a back alley somewhere.'

'Roger, Sir.' a disembodied female voice replied over the radio. 'Charlie Alpha One is only two minutes away from the country park. Charlie Alpha Three is near Badgers Halt and moving towards the Red Hills.'

'Tell Charlie Alpha Three to stay near Badgers Halt.' James commanded firmly. 'That's the only route from the Red Hills to the motorway. I don't want him escaping that way.'

'Roger, Sir.' the voice replied, 'but no joy on the helicopter. It's out of action for maintenance.'

James cursed his luck under his breath.

Daye had only just completed her police driving course, but she had passed with high marks and was now controlling the speeding police car like a veteran. In and out of the traffic she weaved, taking corners at high speed in her hurry to reach the Red Hills Country Park.

'Where about in the park are we heading for, Sir?' She asked tentatively, her eyes never leaving the road.

'The picnic area,' James replied. 'Know it?'

Daye nodded slightly.

A cyclist, without looking, suddenly rode out of a side street causing a recovery vehicle to swerve to avoid him putting his truck on a head on collision course with Daye. She braked violently, but then accelerated quickly, squeezing the police car between a parked car and the red and white recovery vehicle.

That was lucky, thought Daye thankfully, *that truck had a vehicle on the back.*

Daye then put the incident out if her mind as she once again concentrated on the road and the next bend. This was the turn into Dorchester Drive. She braked sharply to take the ninety degrees turn and then accelerated quickly up to eighty miles an hour for the almost straight run to the park gates. Once off the road and through the gates of the park, Daye slowed down to consider the gravel driveway which led to the picnic area. As she made her final braking for the car park, she could see that Charlie Alpha One was already on the scene.

A uniformed woman police constable was with the crying victim, a man's coat about her shoulders to cover her modesty; her daughter, the blood-stained slip around her neck, clasped tightly in her arms.

A male sergeant, late forties and overweight, approached the two detectives as they got out of their vehicle.

'Same MO as the others' Sir,' He stated huskily, and then pointed to the elderly man stood close by, his faithful German shepherd beside him. 'Fortunately, this man was walking his dog and was able to help the woman. She's a Caroline Bamber who only bought the car a couple of months ago.'

'Where was it bought from?' James demanded to know.

'Tattersall's of Brymington, sir.'

'What about the child?' Daye suddenly interrupted the uniformed sergeant, clearly worried about the child's welfare.

'She's called Lucy. She's got a deep cut to her throat, but I don't think it is serious.' He replied, his voice heavy with concern for the little girl. 'There's an ambulance on its way. It should be here soon.'

'What are you doing about this maniac?' A foreign sounding voice demanded to know. 'You should be out chasing him not stood around discussing the weather.'

Both detectives turned to face the elderly man who had approached them quietly.

'This is Mr. Filapowicz.' the sergeant announced by way of an introduction. 'He's a Pole.'

'I am British citizen.' Mr. Filapowicz corrected the sergeant indignantly. 'I came to Britain as a young man over seventy years ago. I was proud to fight alongside the brave British Tommies that were standing up to Hitler.' He then turned to face James and announced with immense pride in his voice. 'I fought at Arnhem.'

Daye smiled at the old man, but it was not a condescending smile. This frail old man, with white hair and a frame that looked like a slight draught would bowl him over, still had the fire and the spirit that symbolised the Polish soldier of the Second World War. If his physical strength could have matched his spirit, the police would not be needed to catch this maniac; this old soldier would have done that himself.

'What can you tell us about him, Mr. Filapowicz?' Daye asked politely.

'He's a girly boy.' He spat contemptuously, his Polish accent still strong after all these years. 'He screamed like big girl when Sosabowski bite him.'

Sosabowski? Daye looked at the German shepherd sat quietly at the feet of his master. The dog looked happy and contented, hard to imagine that it would bite anyone. Mind you, as an experienced police officer, Daye was fully aware that looks could be deceptive.

'When he drove away,' James asked the old soldier, 'did he drive straight back to the main gate?'

'No.' Mr Filapowicz bellowed angrily. 'Why you no listen?' He pointed firmly towards the track in the trees. 'I already tell sergeant he drove down there, towards school.'

'There's an exit down there, Sir.' the sergeant added quickly. 'It's next to the school gates.'

'Right, we'll take a look.' James announced slowly, turning to Mr. Filapowicz. 'Thank you for your help, sir. If you could make a statement to the sergeant here, we'd be most grateful.'

'You're welcome.' Mr Filapowicz replied, his sincerity obvious and clear. 'But let me give you advice.'

'Yes, Sir?' James replied innocently.

'Stop this man from hurting other women. When you catch him cut his balls off; you'll find it's very effective.'

Daye struggled to stop herself from laughing, not so much for the advice but more for the look of surprise on her superior officer's face. James was clearly not expecting that. Mind you it was good advice but, unfortunately, totally illegal.

The two officers got back into their unmarked police car. As she headed for the gravel track that led to the farmhouse museum, she saw out of the corner of her eye that Mr. Filapowicz was now telling the sergeant how to do his job. *Good for you*, thought Daye with a smile, *you tell him*.

The gravel track was narrow, barely the width of a car, and crowded in on both sides by trees and bushes. Ruts cut into the gravel showed where the fleeing Range Rover's tyres had gouged into the track in its haste to escape. Daye went more slowly and carefully.

'That Mr. Filapowicz was a nice man.' She suddenly said casually, but without taking her eyes of the track.

'I suppose so.' James reluctantly agreed. 'I could just imagine him being quite a character in his youth.'

'Strange name for his dog, though.' She uttered quietly. 'What on Earth is a Sosabowski?'

'It's a man not a what.' corrected James, 'General Sosabowski was the commander of the Polish forces at Arnhem. Mr. Filapowicz was obviously very proud to have served under him.'

Daye nodded her head and thought better of making any comment.

'There's the farmhouse car park.' Daye said instead, pointing slightly to the left of them as the track approached the fork in the road.

'Where does that lead too?' James asked inquisitively, pointing to the track off to the right.

'I think that goes through the trees and behind the school.' She replied carefully but sounding none too sure of her facts. 'I think it comes out on the Badgers Halt Road.'

'Well, we've got that covered anyway.' James announced

Daye suddenly stopped as she was about to enter the car park. Both officers got out of the car and looked at the gravel on the ground. Two tyre tracks had deeply gouged the gravel and thrown some of it into the nearby trees.

'He entered the car park too fast.' James remarked, kneeling to have a closer look at the tracks.

'He did more than that, Sir.' Daye added to his remark, pointing to a smear of green paint on a tree next to the car park entrance. 'He must have lost control of the Range Rover as he entered the car park.'

'Much damage would you say?'

'Not really, Sir' She replied casually. 'It looks like a glancing blow.'

'Drive to the school gates.' James ordered.

Daye restarted the car and drove across the gravel car park, exiting on the other side on the track which led to the school gates.

'Stop the car a minute.' James suddenly ordered, indicating with his finger a group of schoolboys with their teacher checking some instruments on the school lawn.

'Excuse me.' James called over to the teacher, a young woman in her early twenties dressed in a stylish blue and green trouser suit. She approached him when he showed her his badge as he exited the car. Some of the boys, obviously curious, followed her over.

'Did anyone see a green Range Rover leave by this gate in the last thirty minutes or so?' James asked the teacher but was obviously asking the group of blue uniformed clad thirteen-year-old boys as well.

The teacher looked at the boys, but they all shook their heads. She then replied that she had not seen anything either.

'I saw a recovery truck leave about twenty minutes ago.' One bespectacled youngster offered.

'That's not a Range Rover though, is it? Moron!'

'Tommy.' The teacher said reproachfully. 'That's enough of that. Frankie was trying to be helpful.'

'Where did this recovery vehicle come from?' Daye asked the bespectacled boy.

'From the car park, of course,' he answered arrogantly, as though it could not have come from anywhere else.

'O yea it did,' another boy confirmed. 'I saw it too. It had a car on the back under some tarpaulin. It wasn't fastened down very well but I think that car was green.'

'It was a Range Rover.' Frankie suddenly shouted. 'I recognised the shape.'

'What colour was the recovery vehicle?' James asked Frankie urgently. 'Was there a name written on it?'

'It was white with a broad red stripe across the middle.'

'Was there any writing on it?' James prompted, 'such as a name?'

'The writing was blue, I think.' The second helpful boy offered, but not too convincingly, 'or maybe black. It was too far away to tell.'

'Thanks.' James shouted as he turned away to speak urgently on the radio.

Daye turned despondently after him.

'The bastard must have had a recovery vehicle waiting for him in that car park.' James uttered angrily to himself as Daye got in the car beside him. 'If he's slipped onto the motorway..........'

'He's back towards town,' Daye announced, just as James picked up the microphone to radio into control. He looked quizzically at her. 'We nearly hit the damn thing getting here. That boy has just described the recovery vehicle that I just managed to avoid.'

'That was twenty minutes ago.' James shouted, putting the microphone down. 'That bastard could be anywhere by now. There's God knows how many garages and lockups in town. We've lost him again.'

James picked up the microphone again, but this time not as fast as before. As he radioed the latest information into control, Daye felt dejected and low. It was not her fault that the woman's attacker had got away, but she had been within shouting distance of him. If she had not been such a good driver, they would almost certainly have collided, and the pervert would have been caught. But they had not collided, and the pervert was, once again, at large and free to strike again. Daye was more determined than ever that this man was going to be caught.

CHAPTER
TEN

Jessica bit her lip as she sat in her white Toyota parked opposite the detached Tudor style house that was the home of the Conway's. She was still not sure that this was a good idea, but she had to know about Ann Walker's involvement in this affair. Jessica's suspicions had sprung to life the moment she set eyes on her at Jack Manning's funeral. She particularly had to know had she ever met Benny, although she doubted if John Conway would be able to answer that question. But he would, no doubt, be able to tell her what connection, if any, Ann had with the late Jack Manning. *Why had she been with the Conway's directly behind the coffin?* Jessica, after thinking about that, also began to wonder *if Ann Walker stood to benefit from Jack's death.* It was a cold thing to think about but, then again, Jessica understood Ann Walker was a cold person.

The rain had momentarily stopped when she plucked up the courage to finally get out of the car and approach the front door. Jessica made sure her appearance looked all right and respectful; so, she wore the same clothes that she had worn yesterday at the Chapel of Remembrance. Her dark hair was short but bushy and looked extremely neat and tidy without the aid of her comb; whilst her makeup was only light and pale; she never liked to overdo the makeup anyway. She declared herself ready as she was about to cross the road to approach the house with the garden gnomes on the neatly cut front lawn.

The front door of the house suddenly opened. John Conway emerged wearing an oversized gabardine and carrying an umbrella. He looked first at the sky before folding the umbrella up and placing it under his left arm; he then stood erect and took in a deep breath. With long strides that befitted a tall man, he marched to the front gate and turned left towards town. Jessica took a deep breath as well, although not as deep as John Conway's, before running across the road to intercept him.

'Excuse me, Mr. Conway.' She shouted merrily, not wishing to alarm him by sounding like just another reporter. He must be fed up with giving interviews by now, Jessica had reasoned.

'Yes?' John Conway called back, stopping in his tracks to allow Jessica to catch up with him.

'Sorry to bother you.' Jessica said sweetly, putting on her most engaging smile. 'But I just wanted to say how sorry I was for what happened to Mr. Manning.'

'That's very kind of you.' John replied kindly, although his face remained as solemn looking as normal. 'Did you know him?'

'Only slightly, I'm afraid.' Jessica lied, for she had never met him. 'He used to coach chess to my younger brother, that's how I met him. He was a nice man.'

Every word a lie and Jessica felt ashamed of herself for saying those words, but she needed to begin a conversation with John Conway.

'I was at the Chapel of Remembrance yesterday,' Jessica continued, glad to be saying something that was true. 'I saw you lead the procession of mourners behind the coffin. That must have been very sad for you.'

Of course, it was sad, you silly cow!!!! Jessica thought angrily at herself, *it was a bloody funeral!!!!*

'Yes.' John said unsmiling although he was not unkind. But he did turn away from her. 'Well, I must be on my way now.'

'Could I just ask you one thing?' Jessica asked firmly, although she hoped that she did not sound rude. John stopped and looked at her waiting for her question. 'Was that Ann Walker that walked into the Crematorium alongside you? Only I once used to know her and wasn't sure if it was her or not.'

'Yes, it was.' John confirmed, his voice beginning to show signs of irritation, 'although she now calls herself Anne-Marie De Wynter. Somewhat pretentious, of course, but that's her choice.'

Anne-Marie De Wynter thought Jessica with as much astonishment as she could muster. *Pretentious is right, and how much like Ann Walker to think of a name like that.*

'I thought it was.' Jessica suddenly blurted out. 'I hadn't seen her since school days, you see. We used to be in the same class at Red Hills High School. She was one of my best friends. But I didn't know that she was related to Jack Manning.'

'Jack was her uncle.' John said, looking at his watch as though he really wanted to move on, 'only in an honorary capacity, of course. Ann's father and Jack used to be firm friends in happier times.'

'Uncle Jack!!!' Jessica tried to sound as though she had heard the name before, which, of course, she had not. 'She used to talk about an Uncle Jack and his coin collection. Was she talking about Jack Manning?'

'Of Course, she was.' John snapped. 'And I really must be going now.'

'Didn't she use to help him with that collection?' Jessica probed, hoping for anything to come back by way of information.

'She occasionally helped Jack buy items for it when she was younger.' He snapped again, once again looking impatiently at his watch. 'And now she has been rewarded for her help. Jack has left that collection to her in his will. And now I really must go. Goodbye.'

'Bye.' Jessica said mildly to the back of John Conway as he turned hurriedly on his heels and headed towards town.

So, she does gain something, thought Jessica with satisfaction. *That stolen coin collection that went missing now actually goes to her, and it's worth a few thousand. She really has been up to something.* It was now time to see what Jimmy MacGregor had to say for himself.

One phone call on her mobile was enough to find out where Jimmy MacGregor was. His wife was certain that he was down at the allotment, and from the tone in her voice Jessica got the impression that he had better not be anywhere else. So, Jessica drove to the canal side allotments, a smile on her face at the thought of a hen-pecked Jimmy MacGregor.

It was mid-afternoon when she walked through the allotments after parking her car next to Jimmy's dark blue Rover, the only other car on the car park. The weather was a lot drier than the day of the funeral, but large puddles were scattered all over the allotments and Jessica had to leap over two particularly large ones to reach Jimmy's shed.

Jimmy had his back to her as she approached the blue and white structure; he seemed to be doing something to the door hinges.

'Hello, Jimmy.' she announced confidently, causing Jimmy to turn around suddenly, dropping the screwdriver that he was holding.

'Oh Hello, Jessica.' he replied, his voice full of surprise but lacking any enthusiasm for seeing her. 'What brings you here?' Jimmy bent down to pick up the screwdriver, and then pointed at the hinges. 'Benny was supposed to have done this while I was on holiday.'

'What do you know of Anne-Marie De Wynter?'

Jimmy turned suddenly to face Jessica, his eyes were wide, and his lips moved but no words left his mouth.

'Cat got your tongue, Jimmy?' Jessica said deliberately with heavy sarcasm, as she entered the shed and made to sit down in the one armchair in the room.

Jimmy followed her into the shed.

'I've asked you a question, Jimmy.' She said firmly as she took her seat in the armchair, 'why no answer?'

'What's going on here?' He demanded to know indignantly.

But his bravado and bluster meant nothing to Jessica. She repeated her question.

'What do you know of Anne-Marie De Wynter?' And then added venomously, 'or do you call her Ann Walker?'

Jimmy stood in the doorway of the shed looking part angry and part frightened. Now Jessica's heart missed a beat;

she suddenly realised that Jimmy was blocking her only exit from the shed. She had foolishly walked into a cul-de-sac and trapped herself. Now she would have to see how good she was at bravado.

'What's she to you?' Jimmy demanded to know.

'Why are you not answering my question, Jimmy?' countered Jessica. 'Got something to hide? Like an affair maybe?'

Jimmy was clearly stunned and said nothing. He merely looked wide eyed at Jessica and bit his lower lip.

'You told Aunt Julie that you had never heard of Jack Manning.' Jessica said accusingly, hoping that she was not being too strong. 'Yet you were at his funeral yesterday and left in your car with Anne-Marie De Wynter, Jack's niece. You then took her to the picnic area of the Red Hills Country Park. Do you want me to go on?'

Jimmy was now more than stunned; Jessica was afraid but trying not to show it. Had she gone too far? But Jimmy did nothing but leaned against the door frame and looked sorry for himself.

'How did you know?' he asked feebly, looking like a shadow of a man instead of a great lover that he had tried to be by trying to keep two women happy. He looked like a trapped rat with nowhere to turn.

'You're not as clever as you think you are.' Jessica said, adding just a little contempt for effect. 'What I want to know is this, what was Ann's involvement with Benny?'

'Benny?' Jimmy replied with surprise as though it was a strange question to be asking. 'They didn't have any involvement at all with each other.'

'Don't tell me they never met.' Jessica shouted angrily, trying to force Jimmy to reply, whilst hoping within her heart that she did not push him too far. 'Now what was their involvement with each other?'

'They had not been involved with each other.' Jimmy answered defiantly, but then added meekly. 'I had an affair with Anne-Marie last year. We used to meet here and that is where she met Benny. But there was no involvement. Benny was outside doing the gardening while we were inside............'

'........getting friendly?' Jessica offered sarcastically, finishing off Jimmy's sentence for him.

'Something like that,' He conceded, 'but other than that they never met each other.'

'Then how did Benny know Jack Manning?' Jessica demanded to know. 'Who just happened to be the uncle of your girlfriend, the man that he is accused of murdering?'

Jimmy shook his shoulders and despite detailed probing by Jessica could not explain how Benny had known Jack Manning.

'I take it your wife doesn't know of your little affair?' Jessica suddenly changed tactics, trying to catch Jimmy off guard.

Jimmy meekly shook his head.

'No.' he said like a frightened little boy. 'And she mustn't know either. I've got too much to lose.'

'Benny has lost his liberty.' Jessica argued, her voice sounding contemptuous of Jimmy. 'Isn't that losing more than you could lose?'

Jimmy did not answer. Jessica got up to leave.

'You'll keep this conversation to yourself?' he pleaded to her as she prepared to walk out through the door. 'I've nothing to do with Jack Manning's murder, so why should I be dragged into it?'

Now it was Jessica's turn to say nothing. She left the shed with one last look of contempt at Jimmy MacGregor.

CHAPTER
ELEVEN

'Somebody wants to see me?' James Buchan asked the desk sergeant at reception.

'Mr. Filapowicz, sir.' The sergeant replied, pointing to the elderly man sat in the corner, the faithful Sosabowski lying at his feet.

James smiled as he saw the old man. Sosabowski sat up and wagged his tail alerting the old man to the presence of the Detective Inspector who was walking over towards them.

'Inspector Buchan,' the old man said in greeting, rising slowly to his feet.

'Mr. Filapowicz.' The D.I. replied, 'and Sosabowski.'

James offered his hand to the German shepherd who licked it gladly, giving James's permission to stroke his ears which James laughingly did.

'You remembered his name.' Mr. Filapowicz said admiringly. 'Not many people can.'

'It's my job to remember, Mr. Filapowicz.' James replied, 'now. You wanted to see me?'

'I have a gift for you from Sosabowski.' Mr. Filapowicz said proudly, offering James a small polythene bag which he tentatively took hold off and examined. There was a small piece of torn material inside, dark blue in colour, and it looked wet and chewed. 'I found it stuck between his teeth after you had left.'

James King's eyes lit up. The material was from the track suit of the woman's attacker. James turned to the desk sergeant and handed him the polythene bag.

'Get that down to the lab quickly.' He ordered in his most urgent sounding voice. 'And I want the results back yesterday.'

'You heard the order.' The desk sergeant shouted to the young, uniformed woman police constable stood behind him. With a surprised look on her face, she took the bag and disappeared behind a collection of desks and filing cabinets that were stacked behind her.

'Thank you, Mr. Filapowicz.' James said sincerely.

'No.' Mr. Filpowicz corrected. 'Thank Sosabowski.'

'Thank you Sosabowski.' James obliged the old man with a smile as he patted the German shepherd on the head. Sosabowski just licked Geoff's hand and loved the attention.

Detective Sergeant Daye Durham said 'Thank you' at the end of her phone conversation as James rushed back into the office. He hastily told her of the torn piece of fabric that Mr. Filapowicz had brought in, ending with the order that she was to ring the lab herself and reinforce his order to get the results to him urgently. Daye immediately did as she was ordered.

James stroked his chin, the stubble reminding him that he had not shaved that morning. But his thoughts were on the torn track suit; *had the balaclava man been injured by the German shepherd? Was there blood on the torn piece of fabric?*

'Do you think it is worth checking the hospitals?' Daye asked tentatively, putting the phone down after talking to the lab where the torn fabric had been taken. 'He may have needed a tetanus jab.'

'Good idea.' James agreed absentmindedly, his thoughts clearly on another aspect of the case. 'But I'm more concerned with this recovery vehicle. Has he used one before?'

'I would think so.' Daye said firmly, sitting back in her chair and looking at her superior officer. 'That would easily explain why these cars are just disappearing into thin air. No trace has ever been found of them.'

James nodded his head in agreement. He stood, hands on hips, beside the window.

'What did you find out about that red and white truck?'

Daye sat forward again and studied the notes in her notebook. She brushed the hair away from her face; a gesture that James noticed. He liked her dark hair the way it was now, free from the ponytail and cascading down over her shoulders. With her dark blue trouser suit contrasting with the white blouse that she wore; James could well imagine her as a successful businesswoman rather than a Detective Sergeant in a provincial force's CID

'Only three companies in this part of Lancashire have recovery vehicles that match the description of the one that we are looking for.' Daye said efficiently, and without looking up towards where her Superior was standing looking at her in an unprofessional manner. 'I've contacted all three and they are going to check their logs to see if any one of their vehicles has been used for a non-authorised purpose.'

James belatedly grunted his approval. He was getting annoyed with himself for not listening with proper attention to his sergeant. *Yes*!!, he chided himself, *Daye Durham is your sergeant so keep your mind on the job in hand.*

Daye looked at him awaiting a comment or two.

'What are the three companies?' James asked half-heartedly, trying to force himself to stop thinking about Daye Durham the woman and more of Daye Durham the efficient detective sergeant.

'Rishton's,' she said firmly, consulting her notes once again. 'Farrimond's, and Tattersall's. And that could be embarrassing if it was one of theirs.'

'Why?'

'Tattersall's do a lot of recovery work for us.' Daye replied half smiling. 'But all three are reputable companies. If someone has borrowed one of their vehicles without permission, they'll let us know.'

'Now the question is,' James said thoughtfully, turning his gaze away from Daye and towards the window where the view was not as attractive but certainly less distracting. 'Is the balaclava man working alone or with someone else?'

Daye sat bolt upright, thinking intently as her flared nostrils gave her away once again.

'You're thinking of the timings, aren't you?' She politely asked.

'If he parked that recovery vehicle on the farmhouse museum car park before he went to Turner's hyper market,' James replied thoughtfully. 'How long would it be parked there before he was able to load a car onto the back of it?'

Daye smiled as though she had been thinking along the same lines.

'It must be at least an hour,' she said carefully, standing up and moving towards the coffee machine, 'perhaps even longer.'

'And what of the previous cars that he has stolen?' James persisted, turning to face Daye and nodding his head to her unasked question of 'would you like a cup of coffee?' 'If he has parked that same recovery vehicle close by on each occasion, why has nobody noticed it before? A driverless recovery vehicle is not exactly a common truck to see parked in quiet places. Surely somebody would have noticed it.'

'I think that suggests that someone else was driving it.' Daye answered, pouring James his coffee. 'And driving it to wherever it was needed, arriving at about the same time as the woman was being attacked. That way it is only on the scene for the bare minimum of time.'

'That's exactly what I think.' James agreed, taking the offered cup of coffee from Daye, but trying desperately to avoid eye contact with her. 'But what's the purpose of the sex attacks on the women?'

Daye looked confused for the moment.

'Sir?' she asked in bewilderment. 'Surely he was attacking them for some form of sexual gratification.'

'Was he?' James asked tantalisingly. 'Or was he merely delaying them?'

Daye stood back and looked closely at her superior officer. She clearly did not understand his thinking on the matter.

'It takes time to load a recovery vehicle.' James began to explain, slowly moving towards his desk to take his seat. 'The vehicle must be loaded, secured, covered with a tarpaulin, and then driven slowly away to not arouse suspicion. By deliberately traumatising the victim, he buys that time. He leaves them naked and confused. That way they are unable to raise the alarm quickly.'

'So, we end up looking for a car instead of the recovery vehicle.' Daye remarked, her voice strained and full of astonishment. 'It's still sick what he does to them.'

'I Agree.' James conceded. 'But look what happened yesterday? By the time we found out that the Range Rover was not on the road but on the back of that truck it was too late. The truck had vanished. I take it that there are no fresh reports on it, are there?'

Daye shook her head.

'There is something that I have been thinking about though.' It was Daye's turn to tantalise. She approached the wall map beside James' desk. James turned his swivel chair around to look at what she was pointing at. Her long index finger was pointing to the farmhouse museum. 'There are two exits from that car park. One leads to the exit next to the school gates, the one they chose to leave by. A strange choice, especially as it was a school day, and they were likely to be spotted by pupils and teachers.'

'And they were.' James confirmed.

'Exactly, Sir,' Daye continued. 'So why not use the other exit? That leads through the trees behind the school. They wouldn't be seen on that track.'

'So why didn't they use that track?'

'Because they were in a hurry,' Daye answered firmly. 'And I think they took the wrong exit by mistake and found themselves at the school gates.'

'Sosabowski rattled them.' James commented, but added sharply, 'where does that other track lead to?'

'It leads to the Badgers Halt Road, Sir.' Daye pointed to the thin black line that led to the village of Badger's Halt. 'That, of course, leads to the motorway.'

'Which they didn't attempt to reach,' James said thoughtfully, looking intently at the map.

'No, Sir.' Daye agreed. 'They turned towards town. But they could have re-joined this road just before reaching Belmont, and then headed away from Badgers Halt.'

James stood up to get a closer look at the map. The other end of the Badgers Halt Road leads through the village of Brymington before disappearing into the Lancashire countryside.

'And what's at Brymington?' James asked, half suspecting that Daye already knew.

'Tattersalls for a start.' She replied earnestly. 'And they have red and white recovery vehicles.'

James started to stroke the stubble on his chin as he thought.

By God!!!, he thought earnestly to himself, *Daye's got something. But there is one key element missing.*

'Why target those women in particular?' He suddenly asked, 'And how were they targeted?'

'All the cars are fairly new, Sir.' Daye offered. 'Maybe he was looking for women with particular cars.'

'Or cars with particular women drivers.' James replied, trying desperately to understand the balaclava man's thinking. 'What is he targeting first? Is it the car or the women?'

'Going off what you said earlier, Sir, I think it has got to be the car.'

'It has to be.' James enthused. It was now beginning to make sense. 'He first targets the type of car he wants. Then he looks for a woman driver who has that type of car. Then he looks for a woman driver who has that type of car and a child. He then uses the child to force the woman to drive to some lonely spot; sexually assaults her to deliberately traumatise her so that he can escape with the car he's targeted in the first place.'

'It sounds so cold and mechanical.' Daye said, clearly not happy about James' logical thinking. 'That makes the sex attack nothing more than a means to an end. That's worse than sick.'

'I totally agree.' James admitted, sickened that someone could sink as low as the balaclava man had in deliberately traumatising his helpless victims just so he could steal their cars. 'We have got to find out how he does it? Something must link those seven cars that have been stolen.'

'They're all fairly new.' Daye offered.

'But they're different makes and models.' James countered, adding in his most authoritative voice. 'Concentrate on that angle. I want to know everything about those cars.'

CHAPTER
TWELVE

★ ★ ★ ★

Anne-Marie sat behind her desk in front of the managing director's office and shook her head. She grimaced as she read of the previous night's editorial in the local paper about the man now known as the 'balaclava man'.

He's depraved, she thought bitterly to herself, *assaulted with a foreign object? How awful. If this has been going on for four years, why haven't the police done something by now? Lazy buggars!!! And that description sounds distinctive, a dark blue track suit with matching balaclava? Surely someone has noticed that.*

Suddenly there was a tap on the outer office door. It opened slowly as Melanie the office junior of Afro Caribbean origin, of slim build and no more than seventeen years old, stuck her head around the door.

'Is it all right to come in?' She asked meekly, as though afraid that Anne-Marie would bite her head off.

Anne-Marie smiled kindly at her; she liked Melanie.

'Of course,' she said firmly, but not unkindly. 'Just knock and enter. You only must knock and wait at Mr. Ashcroft's door.'

Melanie smiled a bright smile as she looked at the inner office door. Someone had used black paint, and not very good paint as it had partially run, to mark the glass of the door with the words 'Mr. R. Ashcroft, Managing Director.' The smile slowly disappeared. Melanie had been given the task of contacting maintenance to have the painting redone. She had forgotten.

'It's all right, Melanie.' Anne-Marie said softly, guessing what was on Melanie's mind. 'I've contacted them myself this morning.'

Melanie gave a relieved smile.

'Sorry.' She uttered softly, entering the room timidly and offering Anne-Marie a manila folder that she was carrying.

Anne-Marie took it; briefly looked at the title; and handed it back to Melanie.

'File it with the rest, will you?' she asked the office junior. 'But before you do that. Get me a cup of tea, will you? I'm gagging here for a brew.'

Melanie smiled brightly before putting the envelope down on the desk and disappearing quickly out of the door.

Anne-Marie looked at the editorial again; grimaced again, and then put the paper down. The outer office door opened. Anne-Marie looked up and smiled as Jimmy MacGregor entered, although she had to smile to herself at the surreptitious way that he crept into the office.

'Where is he?' he whispered, pointing towards the Managing Directors door.

'A meeting,' she answered firmly, 'but you're one of his foremen. You are allowed to come in here.'

'I know. I know.' He replied anxiously, closing the door quietly behind him. 'But I had to see you on your own.'

'What?' Anne-Marie gasped in mock surprise. 'You want to see me in the middle of the morning? Whatever would Susan think?'

'Knock it off.' Jimmy shouted angrily, moving towards Anne-Marie, his hands and body clearly shaking with fear. 'I need to talk to you.'

'Get a grip, Jimmy.' She shouted back at him. 'What on Earth is the matter with you?'

'She knows. 'He blurted out, the words falling awkwardly off his tongue. 'She knows.'

'Who knows?' Anne-Marie demanded to know, the irritation in her voice unmistakable. 'Stop talking gibberish and try English instead. Who knows? And what does she know?'

'Jessica.' Jimmy could barely bring himself to say her name. 'Benny's cousin. She knows.'

'Benny's cousin?' Anne-Marie echoed slowly, raising her shoulders as well as her eyebrows in order to reinforce her puzzlement, 'Jessica who? I didn't know Benny had a cousin.'

'Jessica Morris.' Jimmy spat as he began to pace the floor. 'She's about your age. She's been like a big sister to him. Anyway, she knows about us and might just tell Susan.'

Anne-Marie thought for a few seconds. Benny had indeed mentioned a 'Jessica' to her, although she would not, of course, admit that to Jimmy. But as to being a cousin, or indeed a 'big sister' for that matter, Benny had not made that clear to her. She had thought him a boy living alone, trying to prove his independence, and not a boy with a 'big sister' looking after him. This changes things, and especially after hearing the surname 'Morris.' Anne-Marie recognised the name, particularly as Jimmy had just said that it belonged to a girl of Anne-Marie's own age. She had once gone to school with a girl named Jessica Morris.

'What does this Jessica want to make her keep quiet about us?' Anne-Marie demanded to know, a steely hardness entering her voice.

'She wanted to know exactly what your involvement with Benny was.' Jimmy replied half-heartedly. 'Naturally I replied that there was no involvement between you two. She wouldn't believe me though.'

'Does this Jessica know me?'

'She's seen you certainly.' Jimmy replied quickly, the frightened nervousness in his voice quite clear. 'And she knows that you used to be called Ann Walker. She followed us from the funeral to the Red Hills. What are we going to do if she tells Susan?'

A cold hand gripped Anne-Marie's heart. Jessica Morris the 'Big Sister' was Jessica Morris the schoolgirl that Anne-Marie had once known. She remembered her as a snobbish girl who disapproved of her games with the boys, especially one boy, Joshua Anderson. Jessica had levelled certain accusations against her but, fortunately, no proof. Nevertheless, a strange uneasiness remained between then until the day of their final exams; they never saw each other again after that. Now Jessica Morris was back, and Anne-Marie would, once again, face the accusations that would inevitably follow; Jessica Morris now had a new cause instead of Joshua Anderson; she was 'big sister' to her cousin, Benny.

'Do you think it would help if I spoke to her?' she suddenly asked, her voice full of pretend concern for Jimmy. 'After all, you had nothing to do with the murder of my uncle. If I can make her see that then she might decide to not say anything to Susan.'

'Would you do that for me?' Jimmy begged her, a wretched smile on his face that disgusted Anne-Marie. He was only thinking of himself again.

Anne-Marie heard light footsteps in the corridor outside the office; Melanie was returning with her tea.

'I can only do my best, Jimmy.' Anne-Marie said graciously but added with a strong hint of warning. 'But you are going to have to do something yourself if I can't talk her out of talking to Susan.'

'I'll shut her up somehow.' Jimmy blurted out, oblivious to the office door opening behind him. 'Whatever happens I'll make sure Jessica never talks to Susan.'

Anne-Marie said nothing, but her eyes looked beyond Jimmy. Jimmy turned and saw Melanie standing in the doorway holding a fresh cup of tea. Anne-Marie smiled inwardly to herself; Melanie had clearly heard Jimmy's last words.

Daye entered the interview room near the reception of Templegate police station. As she closed the door she smiled at the room's only occupant, Jessica Morris. Jessica smiled awkwardly back. After formal greetings, Daye sat down at the table opposite Jessica.

'What can I do for you, Miss Morris?' She began mechanically, not really wanting to be here as she suspected that Benny's cousin would only be here to plead that the police should do more to find the real killer of Jack Manning because Benny could not have done it. But Daye was wrong.

'I know that Benny has done a terrible thing.' Jessica began, wiping a tear away from her eye. She clearly did not want to be saying such things. 'But I am concerned as to why he has done it.'

'So are we, Miss Morris.' Daye replied. 'But all he says is that Jack Manning was a bad man and deserved what he got. What do you think Benny meant by that?'

'I don't know.' Jessica said softly but added firmly. 'But I think Anne-Marie De Wynter could answer that question for you.'

Daye suddenly sat bolt upright. *Anne-Marie De Wynter? Who's she?*

'You've not heard of her, have you?' Jessica observed, her tone of voice suggesting some form of accusation. 'She's the link between Benny and Jack Manning. She's also inherited that coin collection that disappeared at the time of the murder.'

Jessica then went on to tell Daye all she knew of Anne-Marie De Wynter, or Ann Walker, as Jessica preferred to call her. She left nothing out; Red Hills High School; Joshua Anderson; her games with the boys; her affair with Jimmy MacGregor; the allotment shed; her devious nature; everything. Jessica even added her encounter with MacGregor at the allotment shed just for good measure.

'Mr. Meadows is still at Red Hills.' Jessica added resolutely. 'He can confirm what she was like there.'

Daye wrote down the teacher's name in her notebook.

'How did you get on to Benny so quickly?' Jessica suddenly asked. 'Or shall I tell you?'

Daye waved her hand as though encouraging Jessica to continue.

'You found Jack's body on the Friday. Correct?' Daye nodded her agreement. 'You arrested Benny Saturday morning. Correct?' Daye nodded again. 'Yet there is no apparent link between the two of them. So how did you get on to Benny so quickly?'

'I'm afraid I can't tell you that, Miss Morris.'

'Then I'll tell you, shall I?' Jessica offered, obviously not interested in what Daye's answer would have been anyway. 'You got an anonymous phone call, or some such anonymous message.'

'How did you know that?' Daye probed.

'Because that is the way Ann Walker works.'

The white Toyota was parked outside number 17 Acacia Avenue, the semi-detached home of Benny Gordon's mother. Anne-Marie stood on the opposite side of the road; her brown leather coat pulled tightly about her to keep out the nightly chill. She looked at her watch for the God knows how many numbers of times since she had got here; it was approaching nine thirty. She had been stood outside for nearly two hours; waiting, just waiting. This was her only clue as to where she could find Jessica Morris; Benny had once told her where his mother had lived. So, it was here that she started looking first for Jessica.

Anne-Marie opened the small matching brown handbag that she carried and fumbled for one of the two flasks of coffee that she had inside. She looked for the piece of masking tape that she had put on the cap; it was not there so she withdrew the flask and poured herself a hot cup of coffee. And God it was hot; she felt the reviving liquid flowing through her, its heat rekindling her spirits.

'Goodbye, Aunt Julie.'

Anne-Marie looked up at the sound of the words. *At Last*, she thought, *Jessica is leaving her aunt's house.*

Jessica fumbled for the key to her car and did not notice the figure that crept up behind her.

'Hello, Jessica.' Anne-Marie said, enjoying the look of surprise and shock on Jessica's face as she hurriedly turned around.

'What the hell are you doing here?' Jessica blurted out, her breath erratic and stilted.

'Waiting to have a word with you,' Anne-Marie replied, her voice friendly with not a trace of menace. 'Can we go somewhere to talk?'

Jessica looked suspiciously at Anne-Marie for a few seconds before motioning her head towards the passenger side of the car. Anne-Marie smiled as she walked around the car and calmly got in the passenger seat. Jessica started the engine and slowly drove away.

'Where do you want to go?' Jessica asked, her voice betraying her unease.

'Oh, somewhere nice and quiet.' Anne-Marie replied casually, trying to put Jessica off her guard. 'You choose.'

Jessica drove into the night. Anne-Marie looked at her and smiled in a friendly way towards her, although inside she felt nothing for this interfering bitch!!!

The car park of the cinema multiplex was nearly full of empty cars, their occupants inside the star shaped building probably enjoying the varied movies on offer that night. Jessica parked near the entrance to the building.

'Right, Ann, we're here.' Jessica said coldly. 'What do you want to talk about?'

'Oh, everything I suppose.' Anne-Marie replied, taking out her coffee flask again and pouring herself a coffee. She replaced the flask in the handbag. 'Oh, I'm sorry, Jessica. I'm forgetting my manners. Would you like a coffee? It's a chilly night.'

Jessica did not reply but nodded her head slightly after a few seconds. Anne-Marie placed her cup on the dashboard as she reached inside for the flask and a clean cup. She felt for the piece of masking tape. As her fingers touched it, she gripped the flask tightly and withdrew it and the cup. Slowly she poured the hot liquid into the plastic cup and then, smiling a disarming smile, she handed the drink to Jessica who took it gladly. Anne-Marie smiled to herself as Jessica drank from the cup.

'So how have you been keeping, Jessica?'

'I want to know about you and Benny.'

'Benny is a nice boy.' Anne-Marie said patronisingly, 'but not my type.'

'He has a pulse, hasn't he?' Jessica snapped back, biting her lip quickly.

'I didn't have you marked down as bitchy.' Anne-Marie replied with mock hurt in her voice. 'I shall have to re-appraise my opinion of you.'

'I'm sorry.' Jessica offered, although her apology sounded a lot less than sincere. In fact, her apology sounded drowsy. She put the plastic cup down on top of the dashboard in front of her, but her hand was shaking, and the cup and the coffee fell off the dashboard and onto her lap causing her to cry out as the hot liquid spread over her.

'Careless.' Anne-Marie said sarcastically, continuing to drink her own coffee as though nothing had happened.

But something had happened. Jessica began to breathe heavily, her eyes were wide open, sweat ran down her forehead and temples, and her hands were shaking. Gradually her breathing slowed, as did her shaking; her head began to fall forward onto her chest as her eyelids got heavy; and her body began to sink into her seat and crumple up like a discarded rag doll. She eventually fell into a deep and untroubled sleep, almost a coma with her breathing shallow and regular.

Anne-Marie continued to drink her coffee. She had watched Jessica struggle in vain against the sleeping pills that had quickly overpowered her but had done nothing to help her former school friend, unless, of course, you could call smirking vindictively as doing something.

But was Anne-Marie doing the right thing? Everything had gone well so far; she had proved to herself that it was possible to influence someone to go out and kill another person. It was not that she did not like her Uncle Jack, she loved him, but he had rejected her. Now he had paid the price for his rejection of her. Anne-Marie had waited until she no longer needed him, and then, with some carefully chosen words, had made Benny kill him. And nobody was any the wiser because Anne-Marie had persuaded the lovesick fool, Benny, to keep her secret about her uncle. But it was a secret that did not actually exist; Benny only believed it did.

She had got away with it and Benny was going to pay the price. Anne-Marie had planned it so carefully but had overlooked one serious flaw in her plan: Jessica Morris. Anne-Marie had not even realised that Jessica was on the scene and, with the knowledge gained from Red Hills High School, could seriously have damaged her intentions.

Indeed, Anne-Marie was now fearful that she would join Benny Gordon in the dock and be jointly accused of murder with him. Only Jessica could do that to Anne-Marie.

With a careful look around to see that no one was looking, Anne-Marie pulled Jessica's limp frame over onto the passenger seat. She then slowly, and carefully, took Jessica's place behind the wheel of the Toyota. Anne-Marie took one last look around the car park to make sure that no one had seen her. Once satisfied that no one had, Anne-Marie drove Jessica's Toyota out onto the road.

The drive to Hunter's Quarry took her through Belmont and onto the Badger's Halt Road. Once through Brymington and into the countryside, Anne-Marie heaved a sigh of relief. The quarry was just up ahead on the right.

The night was dark, but at least it was not raining as she drove carefully onto the quarry site. The surrounding hills, shear and badly scared, were like a giant horseshoe that enclosed the quarry with an eerie blackness that was pitch in colour and unnerving. The lake was just ahead, the water deep, black, and cold. It was fed by an underground stream that had swamped the large crater creating the lake and ending the quarrying operations. The site was abandoned now; unused for three years. It was onto a ledge about fifty feet above the water that Anne-Marie drove the Toyota.

Anne-Marie stopped the car at the edge and applied the hand brake. She got out of the Toyota and looked down at the inky blackness below; the water had barely a ripple on it giving it the appearance of thick impenetrable treacle. A lump of emotion came into her throat. But she forced herself to ignore it; Anne-Marie convinced herself that what she had to do was unavoidable.

Jessica was slumped in the passenger seat, her breathing slight and almost inaudible; although, maybe, Anne-Marie just did not want to hear it. She did not want to look at her either as she positioned Jessica behind the steering wheel before releasing the hand brake. She then pushed the white Toyota over the edge.

It fell slowly, as though in a dream, towards the water. Anne-Marie watched; her face a mask of stony calm. The inky blackness suddenly threw up white spouts of water as the Toyota flipped over onto its back as it crashed into the all-embracing darkness of the lake. The car floated for a second or two, its four wheels pointing defiantly towards Anne-Marie. But the defiance was short lived as the black waters flowed over the chassis and pulled it down towards the bottom of the crater. Within minutes, as Anne-Marie watched, the surface of the lake returned to its eerie calmness; a calmness that looked like it had never been disturbed.

Anne-Marie turned her back on the lake and pulled the coat tightly around her. *Jessica may still have been alive as the car hit the water, but she would have known nothing about it*, Anne-Marie thought to herself, trying to sound as though she had been as humane as possible. But how could any murder be described as humane? And murder this was.

Anne-Marie tried to force her mind into a blank; she did not want to think on what she had done. But as she put her hands into her pockets, her heart missed a beat. Where was her handbag? Anne-Marie quickly looked around the ledge, and then with a faint heart at the water of the lake. Her handbag and the two flasks where still in the car. She tried desperately to remember what else was in the handbag as well but could not remember. She hoped that there was nothing incriminating in it. Unfortunately for Anne-Marie there was something incriminating in the handbag, but she had forgotten about it. But then again, who knew that Jessica was at the bottom of the lake? Jessica was gone and so was the evidence. They would never be found; and she would never be connected to her disappearance. Anne-Marie was back in control.

She smiled faintly to herself as she began the long walk, four or five miles? back to Brymington where she would have a late meal at the 'Black Bear' before taking a taxi home.

CHAPTER
THIRTEEN

★ ★ ★ ★

Daye was tying her hair back into a ponytail as James entered the office. She looked casually at him before giving him a relaxed smile. James sheepishly smiled back as he took his seat behind his desk and began rummaging through the paperwork piled high in front of him.

'Have you anything on those cars yet, Daye?' He asked in a not too convincing casual manner.

'Nothing definite, Sir. 'She replied, looking for her notebook on her own desktop which was also covered in paperwork. 'But one thing I have discovered is that although the stolen vehicles were fairly new, they were not bought new.'

'They were all second hand?' James queried, leaning back in his swivel chair as he looked at Daye.

'Yes, Sir.' Daye confirmed, her long fingers thumbing through the pages of the notebook. 'All the cars were bought locally from three different garages. I'm just trying to establish now if there is any connection between those garages.'

'Which garages are they?'

'Smithson's, Holden's and...' Daye held her breath teasingly. 'Tattersall's of Brymington.'

'Tattersall's' James almost shouted as he heard the name. 'They've got red and white recovery vehicles. How many cars were bought there?'

'Three.' Daye replied as she consulted her notes, 'including the Range Rover.'

James stood up and walked towards the window, his right hand stroking his chin. Daye watched him, waiting for either a comment or a command. She had worked with James ever since her transfer to Templegate upon confirmation of her promotion to Detective Sergeant. Daye had wanted to work with D.I. Buchan, he was a well-respected police officer, and she was an ambitious policewoman. Working with him could only do her career prospects good; that had been the original intention, but now as she sat and watched the officer that she admired, even revered, ponder over his next move; her thoughts were not all on the case in hand.

Working so closely with James had enabled Daye to find out a great deal about her work colleague; and what she saw she liked. And it was not so much his ability as a police detective that she liked either; his personal qualities had also gained her admiration. He was thoughtful and, underneath his sometimes-gruff exterior, Daye sensed that he was a caring and loyal person; an ideal husband for someone in fact. *But not for me*, thought Daye despondently, *I'm too busy to have a love life and someone like James Buchan is not going to look twice at me.*

'What about the finance to buy those cars?'

James' question momentarily stunned her out of her daydream. Daye fumbled for her notes.

'There were four different finance companies, Sir.' She said with a slight stammer as she tried to quickly compose herself. 'One was even through a bank.'

'Then it's not the finance.' James announced with certainty. 'That's puts us back with the garages themselves. I think a visit to one is called for.'

Daye smiled and nodded her agreement.

'Tattersall's?' she asked, raising herself from her desk. 'They sold the last vehicle stolen and have red and white recovery vehicles.'

'Yes.' James replied. 'We'll go in my car. It looks like it's ready for a trade in.'

The phone on Daye's desk suddenly rang out. Daye answered it and listened to a short message before saying 'Be right there' and putting the receiver down.

'Mrs. Gordon is in the interview room.' She said, turning to face James who was looking for his car keys in his desk drawer.

'I'll meet you in the car park.' He said authoritatively, picking up his car keys and placing them in his pocket.

Mrs. Julie Gordon was short, plump, and very agitated. She smiled sheepishly at Daye as she entered the interview room and sat opposite her.

'How can I help you, Mrs. Gordon?' Daye began, trying to sound emotionally detached as though not wishing to encourage Julie Gordon to speak. Daye had heard her speak several times already and it was always the same. 'The police have made a big mistake'; 'My son is not a killer.'; 'You've got to find the real person responsible.' Daye had heard it all. She did not wish to hear it again.

'My niece, Jessica, is missing.' Julie Gordon said tearfully.

Oh no, thought Daye angrily to herself. *Is this some sort of family ploy to prove Benny's innocence?*

'I saw Jessica myself on Wednesday.' Daye said dismissively. 'That was only two days ago.'

'I know.' Julie replied, brushing her long unkempt hair away from her reddened eyes. 'She came round that night to tell me what she had said to you. She left my house at about half past nine and has not been seen since. She never went home.'

Was it a ploy? Daye thought carefully, now not so sure.

'Could she not have gone to see friends somewhere?'

Julie violently shook her head as though the suggestion was absurd.

'None of her friends have seen her.' She said firmly. 'I've rung them; Jessica's mother has rung them. We're all concerned about her.'

Daye wrote the details down in her notebook.

'She's not fallen foul of that 'balaclava man' has she?'

Daye looked intently at Julie Gordon; it was a genuinely sincere question. Jessica Morris had apparently gone missing.

'You can relax on that count, Mrs. Gordon.' Daye said confidently, adding a slight smile for effect. 'From what you've told me he is not involved.'

Julie Gordon smiled a reluctant and strained sort of smile; she was not convinced.

'Let me just write down all the details.' Daye continued, her smile encouraging Julie Gordon to reveal all she knew.

Tearfully, but thoroughly, Julie Gordon told Daye everything that had happened over the previous two days. Daye wrote everything down.

'I don't know if it is significant or not, 'Julie Gordon added quietly as though what she was about to say was probably insignificant, 'but Jimmy MacGregor has been asking about Jessica. He rang for her several times yesterday.'

Daye arrived in the car park at the same time as James. They met beside the battered Ford Mondeo that James called his 'Better than the wife'; the reason being that it was more reliable and never answered back.

'What did Mrs. Gordon want?' James asked casually as he unlocked the driver's door of the light grey car.

'Jessica Morris is missing.' Daye replied, the tone of her voice betraying her uncertainty of the accuracy of her answer.

James got into his car and lent over to open the passenger door.

'Is it some sort of ploy?' He asked as he pushed the door open.

'I'm not sure.' Daye answered as she sat down in the passenger seat. 'It's only two days ago that I saw her. Benny's family could be trying something on to make us continue looking into the case but..................'

'But what?' James prompted turning the key in the ignition.

'It's what Jessica came to see me about.' The nostrils of Daye's nose flared as she spoke. 'It was about this woman, Anne-Marie De Wynter.'

'What have you learned about her?' James asked quietly, his eyes carefully watching the flow of traffic on the busy road in front of Templegate.

'Well, the background information we collected on her matches what Jessica told me.' Daye said impassively. 'She was originally called Ann Walker and was a classmate of Jessica's at school.'

'What about any link between Benny and Anne-Marie?'

'At Jimmy MacGregor's allotment you mean?' Daye asked firmly although it sounded more like a statement than a question. 'Jimmy and Anne-Marie both work at the same factory; Ashcroft Fabrications. He's a foreman and she's the personal assistant to Ashcroft himself.'

'So, they must have met there.' James said firmly, edging his car carefully into the flow of traffic.

'Mostly meetings with the boss,' Daye replied. 'But also, at the allotment where Benny helped out on.'

'They didn't meet anywhere else?'

'Apparently not.' Daye said in a slow and careful voice 'But MacGregor is married to the boss's daughter so they would have to be very careful and secretive if they were having an affair. Jessica said that MacGregor confirmed to her that he and Anne-Marie were indeed seeing each other, and they had frequently met at the allotment that Benny helped on.' Daye paused for a moment before adding. 'I would like to follow up on that. Jack Manning apparently didn't know either Benny Gordon or Jimmy MacGregor. But Anne-Marie did know Jack. And she knew Benny. Did she have an affair with Benny as well as MacGregor?'

'That's an interesting possibility.' James said thoughtfully before ordering. 'See what you can find out.'

'And what was MacGregor's relationship with Jessica Morris?'

James looked intrigued but said nothing, waiting for Daye to continue.

'MacGregor has been ringing up after Jessica all day yesterday.'

'Sounds like there is more to this than meets the eye.' James said thoughtfully, 'Keep on top of it and keep me informed.'

Daye nodded her agreement with her superior's instructions but said nothing as James' mobile phone, lying on the dashboard, suddenly gave out a cavalry charge ringtone. Daye smiled as she picked it up.

'It's Ferguson in the lab.' She said mechanically, looking at the dialling number on the phones little screen.

'Good.' James said firmly. 'What's he got to say?'

'Hello?' Daye asked coldly into the phone.

Daye listened impassively while James fired agitated glances at her whilst trying to watch the traffic at the same time. At the end of the phone call, she merely said 'Right, I'll tell him.' before she hung up.

'Ferguson said that there was no DNA on that piece of cloth...' Daye began, sounding as though she was giving an official report.

'Oh Damn!' James responded angrily. 'We needed that DNA.'

'But he has an idea, Sir.' Daye said teasingly to which James' frown of 'get on with it then' prompted her to complete the sentence. 'Ferguson thinks he may be able to identify the track suit manufacturer.'

James smiled in a satisfactory manner. It would be giant stride towards identifying the 'balaclava man' if they could trace him through his distinctive tracksuit.

CHAPTER
FOURTEEN

The drive to Brymington village from Templegate did not take long; maybe twenty minutes or so. It was part of the borough and yet looked like a rustic village with its traditional Post office, Pub, and corner shop. All the houses were terraced and built out of stone instead of brick. If it was not for Tattersall's on the edge of the village the visitor could be forgiven for thinking that he had stepped back into the nineteenth century.

The sales division of Tattersall's was on the left side of the road that lead into Brymington. A single building comprising a glass fronted showroom on the ground floor with offices upstairs lay in the centre of the compound surrounded by various cars and vans, all spotlessly clean and displaying its 'unbelievably low bargain price'

But as James drove his Mondeo onto the forecourt of the sales division, he could not resist looking at the smaller compound on the opposite side of the road. Under the red and white banner of 'Tattersall's of Brymington' were the workshops and service centre of the maintenance division. But in one corner of the compound were parked the objects of James' curiosity, three red and white recovery vehicles with the words 'Tattersall's of Brymington' painted boldly on the doors in dark blue letters.

'What sort of car do you fancy?' Daye asked in a matter-of-fact manner as they got out of the Mondeo, 'anything in particular?'

'Yeah,' James replied quietly as he looked at the vehicles on display. 'One that they haven't got would be nice.'

'Could I help you sir?'

James turned around to see the source of the voice. It belonged to a young, probably early twenties, well dressed and neatly turned-out man with an engaging smile.

'Are you looking for anything in particular?' the young man continued politely.

'Perhaps a Range Rover George,' James replied casually, looking at the name tag attached to the salesman's lapel. Adding quickly as he looked around the crowded motor park, 'but I don't see any unfortunately.'

'We have one over here.' George answered quickly, indicating with his left hand a metallic maroon Range Rover partially hidden at the back of the motor park. As he led James and Daye towards it George continued speaking. 'Would Sir have a vehicle to trade in?'

James pointed to the Mondeo. 'It's been very reliable but is getting a bit old now and is ready for trading in.'

George looked back at the light grey Mondeo that was certainly old and, going by the dents and scratches, was more than slightly battered. 'I'm sure we could do you a good deal, Sir.'

George's engaging smile never faded.

This fellow is a professional, thought James with a slightly cunning smile to himself. *He could sell contraceptives to a eunuch.*

George opened the Range Rover's door and invited James to sit in the driver's seat while he went through his sales pitch about this reliable and well-maintained car.

'Would Sir like a test drive?' George eventually asked when he had finished his well-written and well-rehearsed delivery.

'Is this the only colour that you've got?' James replied catching the salesman momentarily off guard although he quickly recovered.

'This is the only Range Rover that we have in now.' George responded, his engaging smile still intact. 'Was there a particular colour that you wanted?'

'I rather fancied a green one actually.' James replied carefully. 'A friend of mine said you had one in just a few weeks ago.'

'I know which one you mean.' George answered, nodding his head slightly. 'A woman bought it. Range Rovers are one of those vehicles that don't stay in stock long. They are very popular.' James put on a pretend disappointed face until George added. 'Would you like me to find you one if I can?'

As soon as James said, 'If you could I would be very grateful.' George then proceeded to lead James and Daye towards the ground floor showroom and to the tidy desk in the corner.

'Please sit down.' George said politely indicating two comfortable looking chairs that were facing the desk, 'tea or coffee?'

'Oh, thank you.' James replied, 'tea please, milk and no sugar.'

George looked smilingly at Daye who answered. 'The same please but with one sugar.'

'I'll be back in a moment'

James and Daye took their seats in front of the desk which had a computer at one end, two metal trays, one marked 'in' and the other 'out', at the other end, and assorted papers neatly arranged on the desktop between them.

James looked casually towards George who was making the tea at a table on the opposite side of the showroom. 'This should be interesting.' he whispered quietly to Daye, who moved her head closer to James' but said nothing. 'This is the only showroom that Tattersalls' have.'

'Then where is the green Range Rover going to come from?'

'I think we are about to find out.' James answered with a sly smile at Daye.

George returned with two cups of tea which he gave to James and Daye before sitting down behind the desk. 'Let's see what A.V.I.S. has for us.'

James lent forward so that he could see the computer screen as it booted up. A.V.I.S. Associated Vehicle Inventory System designed by Whittingham Computer Systems was coming to life.

George pressed a key on the computers keyboard. 'Here's the search screen.'

The computer was now displaying an input screen that was asking for information on the wanted vehicle.

'Right, Sir.' George said confidently. 'Just give me the details of what you're looking for.'

Make of vehicle, model, colour, age, price; everything that James wanted to know about the green Range Rover went onto the screen.

'Is that it?' George asked James who nodded his answer of 'yes'. George pressed the enter key which immediately cleared the screen to be replaced by a revolving hourglass symbol.

'It's just searching through all the inventory databases of the companies involved with A.V.I.S.'

'How many companies is that?'

George explained that over sixty companies throughout England and Wales had linked their inventories to the A.V.I.S. database. This allowed the other companies to see what stock each one had. And if one company should have a customer that liked another company's vehicle then arrangements could be made to transfer that vehicle to the company with the customer.

'And here we have one green Range Rover down in Oxford.' George declared proudly. 'Would you like it transferred up here so you could have a look at it?'

'This is a very interesting computer system.' James declared, deliberately ignoring George. 'Are there any other local companies involved with A.V.I.S? Smithson's for example?'

'Or Holden's maybe?' Daye quickly added.

'Well both companies are connected with A.V.I.S.' George answered with a rather surprised look on his face.

'Could you show us their inventories?' James asked politely. 'I'm rather curious.'

'I could.' George answered slowly. 'But there wouldn't be any point. Neither of them has a green Range Rover. Otherwise, it would have come up on the screen.' George then added quickly. 'Do you want to have a look at this Range Rover from Oxford?'

James and Daye suddenly stood up

James offered his hand to George who also stood up. 'Thank you for all your help, George.' He said sincerely, adding apologetically. 'I'll have to go home and think about this.'

'I could still get it transferred.......' George began meekly.

'Not today.' James interrupted. 'I'll think about it and let you know.'

James and Daye hurried out of the showroom and returned to the Mondeo. As they buckled themselves into their seats James said to Daye. 'Ring up Templegate.' He began firmly. 'I want to know where Whittingham Computer Systems are based, and I want a contact phone number.'

Daye immediately spoke into her mobile phone as James turned the car around and drove for the exit. But Daye had a surprised look on her face as the Mondeo turned left at the main road and headed towards Brymington. Templegate was in the other direction.

Daye put her mobile phone back into her pocket. She still looked surprised as she looked at James who smiled back at her and said, 'It's nearly lunch time. I'm hungry.'

The 'Black Bear' restaurant and pub was a modest sized, stone-built eatery that was at least several centuries old. Its exterior was brightly coloured without becoming gaudy and hanging flower baskets beside the Tudor style windows lent themselves well to its olde-worlde charm.

James parked the Mondeo on the tarmac covered car park at the side of the 'Black Bear'. He walked slowly with Daye around to the front, over the cobblestones, and through the glass and wood front door into the restaurant.

It was just like he remembered it. The wood was highly polished; the decor warm and inviting. Each table was laid out correctly with a crisp and gleaming white tablecloth with condiments in the centre and neatly arranged knives, forks and spoons around the edge waiting patiently for a hungry customer to arrive. At one end of the spacious dining room was a well-stocked bar; its optics displaying various spirits and wines while the pumps displayed beers from different parts of the world. James had been here many times with his wife, or rather ex-wife, but had not been back since his divorce.

'Mr. Buchan.' a jovial sounding Welsh accent warmly welcomed him to the 'Black Bear. 'We have not seen you for such a long while.'

'Good to see you again, Aled.' James shook the outstretched hand of the tall and well-built Welshman who was smartly dressed in his black trousers, white shirt and black waistcoat. 'I thought it was about time that I came back to see you.'

'I'm very glad you did.' the smiling Aled continued, adding quickly. 'Your usual table is over here.'

Only a few tables had diners, but Aled led James and Daye towards a quiet alcove in the corner, its window having a good view of Brymington village and the green Lancashire hills beyond.

James sat opposite Daye and declined the offered menu with a 'you know what I want, Aled.'

'Good choice, Mr Buchan. And what would the young lady have?' Aled asked politely as he turned towards Daye and offered her the menu.

Daye also declined the menu, asking instead. 'Could I have a plain omelette and side salad please?'

Aled smiled as he wrote down their order in his little black notebook.

'And two 'Specials' as well, Aled.' added James.

Aled courteously smiled at James and Daye as he left them to arrange their meals. Daye looked around the room at the paintings, horse brasses and medieval shields that adorned the walls. Her eyes settled on a large red and white striped shield with a ferocious looking black bear standing in its centre that adorned the wall above the fireplace.

'That's the coat of arms of the Fitzroy family.' James explained quietly. 'They owned the land around here for several centuries.'

Daye listened politely to James' explanation until the ring tone on her mobile phone sounded. She picked it up and listened.

'Here are the two 'Specials' as ordered.' Aled said as he returned to the table carrying two long glasses of amber liquid that were topped with a thin white layer of froth. 'These Indian lagers are very popular.' Aled continued.

James thanked Aled who turned towards the kitchen to check on the preparations for their meals.

Daye put her phone down on the table. 'That was Templegate.' She began quietly. 'Whittingham Computer Systems are a Blackburn based computer company. They're near the football ground at Ewood Park.'

'That's just off junction four of the M65.' James replied thoughtfully. 'That's only about ten or eleven miles from here. Did you get a phone number?'

Daye held up her notebook. 'Of course,' she said smiling at James.

'We'll have our meal first,' James said firmly, 'and then we'll contact them.'

'What about Jessica Morris?' Daye suddenly asked, her face betraying an inner turmoil.

James looked at her and sensed what his D.S. was thinking. *Was her family playing some sort of ploy? Or had something genuinely happened to Jessica?*

'Have you something on your mind?' He asked gently.

'It's this Anne-Marie De Wynter.' Daye began thoughtfully but stopped suddenly as she realised that Aled had quietly approached the alcove and was standing next to the table.

'Oh, I beg your pardon.' Aled said apologetically. 'I didn't mean to eves drop. I only hope Miss De Wynter is not in any trouble.'

'That's ok, Aled.' James said quietly. 'Was there something you wanted?'

'Just to say that your meal will be delayed by a few minutes,' Aled said apologetically.

'Don't worry, Aled.' James replied smiling. 'Your meals are always worth waiting for.'

'Thank you, Mr. Buchan.' Aled said, the tone in his voice indicating that he did not wish to upset a valued customer.

'But I take it,' James continued quickly. 'That you know Anne-Marie De Wynter?'

'Oh yes, Mr. Buchan.' Aled responded just as quickly. 'She is a regular customer. She usually comes here with a young man. She's very popular with the young men.'

James could not help noticing that Aled had a disapproving tone in his voice.

'In what way do you mean 'popular'?' James probed, obviously intrigued by the way that Aled was talking.

'I probably shouldn't say this about a customer,' Aled began quietly. 'But she comes here with different men, and they always pay for the meals.'

'Was she using them?' Daye enquired.

Aled nodded, his face betraying his thoughts on the gullibility of youth.

'When was she last here?' James continued.

'Wednesday night.' Aled quickly replied but added immediately. 'But, oddly enough, for once she was on her own.'

'What time was this?'

'Late.' Aled replied slowly as though carefully thinking. 'Certainly, after ten thirty.' James' ears pricked up at the time. 'And she wanted a meal that she paid for.' Aled made no attempt to hide the surprised and mocking tone in his voice.

'How long did she stay for?' Daye asked.

'Just over half an hour I think, and then I rung for a taxi to take her home.'

'Why did she need a taxi?' James asked in a surprised tone. 'Doesn't she have a car of her own?'

'Yes, of course.' Aled replied. 'But going by the state of her shoes, which were more for fashion than hiking in, she had walked a long way going off the dirty and scuffed marks on them. But I don't think for one minute that she had walked here from Belmont.'

'So where had she come from?' James probed.

'She didn't say.' Aled replied with a shrug of his large shoulders but added quickly as he saw one of his waiters signalling to him from the kitchen door. 'I believe your meals are now ready. I'll just get them for you.'

Aled hurried towards the kitchen.

'Jessica was last seen at 9-30pm by her aunt.' Daye began firmly. 'And just over one hour later Anne-Marie De Wynter enters the 'Black Bear' after having apparently walked here.'

'Jessica Morris had a car, didn't she?' James asked slowly

'She had a white Toyota.' Daye replied solemnly. 'It was last seen on Wednesday night outside her Aunt Julie's home.'

'Wouldn't it be interesting if Anne-Marie and Jessica were found to have met up after Jessica had left her aunt's house?' James said in a tantalizing manner.

Daye smiled and nodded her head. 'It could also explain how Anne-Marie got to Brymington as well.' She said thoughtfully.

'Sorry for the delay.' Aled said apologetically as he delivered James and Daye's meals. He placed the large dinner plate with the omelette and side salad on the table in front of Daye who smiled approvingly. The other large dinner plate was placed in front of James who smacked his lips at the sight of his favourite meal; Steak and Ale pie, chips, two veg, and covered in gravy. *I'm ready for this,* he thought gleefully to himself.

CHAPTER
FIFTEEN

'After 10-00am tomorrow?' Daye said softly into her mobile phone whilst she looked straight into James Buchan's face.

James nodded his head in a silent agreement of the time.

'That will be perfect.' she said firmly. 'And I ask for Mr. Tomlinson?'

Daye smiled as she finished the conversation with Whittingham Computer Systems.

'A pity Tomlinson is away today on business.' Daye said regretfully. 'But he's the man in charge of developing the A.V.I.S. program so we'll have to wait until tomorrow when he gets back.'

'But in the meantime,' James began firmly as he turned on the Mondeo's engine and drove slowly off the 'Black Bear's' car park. 'I think we'll pay a visit to Ashcroft's Fabrications.'

The drive back to Bellingham was uneventful and took James and Daye to within a mile of Templegate.

Ashcroft's Fabrications was inside an old riverside cotton mill that had been disused for many years. The exterior still looked derelict with a mud and gravel car park; blackened brickwork that showed occasional displays of green where moss was growing on the walls; and a large quantity of old red with rust machinery that had been removed from the factory and had been disposed of unceremoniously in a field next to the car park.

The interior, on the other hand, looked clean and tidy with plastic panelled walls, tiled floors, and carpeted office floors.

James and Daye were shown into one such office by a young office junior called Melanie who smiled nervously as she introduced the officers to Anne-Marie De Wynter who was stood behind her tidy wooden desk. After watching Anne-Marie shake hands with the two officers, Melanie slipped quietly out of the office. Anne-Marie asked James and Daye to sit down on two straight backed chairs before she sat down on a more comfortable looking chair behind her desk.

'Reception said you wished to see me?' Anne-Marie asked through a sweet and innocent looking smile.

James looked curiously at this very smartly dressed businesswoman in her matching blue jacket and skirt; her plain white, but gleaming, blouse which was slightly open at the neck; but especially at her right shoe which was jutting out from the side of her desk because she was sat cross legged trying to look comfortable and at her ease. The shoe looked very fashionable with a slightly raised heel and the toe end tapering to a point. *Yes,* James thought decisively to himself, *not the type of shoe to go for a long walk in.*

'We're trying to establish a connection between Jack Manning and his killer, Benny Gordon.' James began softly, looking straight into Anne-Marie's blue eyes which looked straight back at him without flinching. 'We believe you knew both men, Miss De Wynter?'

Anne-Marie smiled before answering. 'Yes, I did.'

'I know you regarded Jack Manning as your uncle,' James continued softly, 'but what was your relationship with Benny Gordon?'

'I didn't have any relationship with Benny Gordon.' Anne-Marie replied carefully but added decisively. 'And I think I know where this is leading too.'

'And where is that, Miss De Wynter?' James probed just as carefully, intrigued at what her answer would be.

'You obviously know about my relationship with Jimmy MacGregor'. Anne-Marie began firmly, almost defiantly. 'We used to meet at Jimmy's allotment shed. Benny was quite often there working outside.'

'So, you knew him quite well?' James probed again, looking carefully at her facial expression which gave nothing away, apart from an obvious dislike of the question.

'I did not know him at all.' Anne-Marie replied firmly with more than a touch of irritation in her voice. 'I barely spoke to him. I was at the allotment to meet with Jimmy and nobody else.'

'But you must have spoken to him, surely?' James continued to probe.

'Hello. Goodbye.' Anne-Marie replied, adding quickly. 'And nothing else.'

'Did Mister MacGregor know about Jack Manning?' James asked quickly, looking for a change of expression on Anne-Marie's face. There was none.

'I may have mentioned his name,' Anne-Marie admitted, 'but only in passing. Jimmy didn't know him and as far as I know, had never met my uncle.'

'Has Jimmy MacGregor ever spoken to you about a woman called Jessica Morris?'

This time there was a change of expression on Anne-Marie's face. James smiled. Anne-Marie had clearly not expected that question.

'Why do you ask that?' Anne-Marie asked quickly, trying to compose herself.

'Just answer the question please, Miss De Wynter.' James replied firmly.

'As a matter of fact, he has.' Anne-Marie replied softly. 'He spoke to me about her only last Wednesday.'

'What did you talk about?' James continued, applying just a little more pressure than before.

'I've got a feeling you already know.' Anne-Marie said defensively. 'But I may as well tell you anyway.'

James said nothing but stared intently at Anne-Marie encouraging her to continue.

'Jimmy came to see me in this very office last Wednesday morning.' Anne-Marie began, slightly biting her bottom lip as though preparing her next words to say. 'He told me that Jessica had somehow found out about his affair with me. I think she was threatening to tell his wife and that was petrifying him. He has rather a lot to lose.'

'Was he expecting you to do something?' James asked quizzically.

'I went to school with Jessica.' Anne-Marie began to explain. 'Jimmy wanted me to persuade her not to say anything to Susan, Jimmy's wife.'

'What did you say to Jessica?'

'I said nothing to her.' Anne-Marie replied in a teasing manner. 'I haven't seen her since our days together at Red

Hills High School. Come to think of it,' Anne-Marie added with a quizzical look on her face. 'I haven't seen Jimmy since Wednesday morning. He rang in sick yesterday and hasn't come into work today either.'

'Did he look ill on Wednesday?' James asked rather nonchalantly as though not really interested in the answer but which he was of course.

'He didn't look ill.' Anne-Marie replied. 'Except for being agitated with Jessica.'

'Who hasn't been seen since Wednesday either,' James said quickly while he eagerly studied Anne-Marie's face for her expression. Strangely, she did not seem surprised at the statement.

Anne-Marie sat quietly in her chair; her eyes shut as though in deep thought. Suddenly she sat bolt upright and reached for the phone on her desk. She did not look at either officer as she spoke into the mouthpiece.

'Will you come in here please, Melanie?'

It was a very nervous and timid looking Melanie who slowly entered the office. James and Daye both stood up together and faced the frightened looking black girl. James smiled a disarming smile at her to reassure her.

'Melanie.' Anne-Marie said softly from behind her desk where she had remained seated. 'Tell these two officers what you heard on Wednesday morning when you entered this office and heard Jimmy MacGregor and I discussing a woman called Jessica.'

Melanie looked at the two officers in turn and then at Anne-Marie.

'You mean when I brought your tea in?' She asked Anne-Marie softly.

'That's correct, Melanie,' was Anne-Marie's firm response.

Melanie turned towards the two officers.

'When I entered the office with Anne-Marie's tea,' Melanie began softly, her voice sounding shaky and frightened, 'I heard Mister MacGregor saying "I'll shut her up somehow. Whatever happens I'll make sure Jessica never talks to Susan.'

'Is that word for word, Melanie?' James asked quietly, not wishing to alarm the still shaking office junior.

Melanie did not reply but nodded her head erratically instead.

'Thank you, Melanie.' Anne-Marie said firmly, but coldly as she rose to her feet. 'You may return to your duties.'

Melanie turned quickly towards the door and left the office both swiftly and silently.

'I can confirm what Melanie has just said.' Anne-Marie said firmly to the two officers but added quickly. 'I can't believe that Jimmy would do anything to make his threat come true though.'

'Can you swear on the bible to that?' James asked pointedly, to which Anne-Marie's stony silence spoke volumes. 'Have you got Mister MacGregor's home address please?'

Anne-Marie wrote the address that James wanted on a page of her notebook and then tore it out and handed it to James who said, 'Thank you.'

James and Daye moved towards the office door while Anne-Marie took her seat again behind her desk. As Daye opened the door, James suddenly turned and faced Anne-Marie.

'Just one more thing, Miss De Wynter,' He asked quietly but firmly. 'Can you tell us where you were on Wednesday evening?'

Anne-Marie looked temporally stunned but quickly returned herself to her normal look of self-assured calmness.

'That's a strange question.' She suddenly said with a half-hearted look of puzzlement on her face. 'What's that got to do with anything?'

'If you would just answer the question, please,' James said firmly but politely.

'I was home alone as it happens.'

'Were you in all evening?'

Anne-Marie did not immediately answer. James could see that she was puzzling over what to say. So, she said nothing.

'You were in the 'Black Bear' on Wednesday night.' James suddenly said, smiling at the look of shock on Anne-Marie's face.

'How did you know that?' Anne-Marie almost shouted sharply.

'Would you mind telling me what you were doing there?' James continued firmly, adding slowly for effect 'Alone.'

Anne-Marie looked angry at first but said nothing until she had slowly composed herself. She suddenly smiled before answering James' question.

'O.K.' she began carefully. 'I was there to meet Jimmy MacGregor. We were going to talk about Jessica. Unfortunately, he didn't turn up, so I ate alone.'

'Why weren't you in your car?'

'I got a taxi down because I was meeting Jimmy. I was expecting him to drive me home afterwards. Now is there anything else you need to know?'

James smiled as he said, 'No thank you.'

Outside the rain was drizzling as James and Daye hurried across the car park to where their car was parked. Once inside the Mondeo, James turned towards Daye.

'What was the name of that teacher at Red Hills High School?'

'You mean the name that Jessica gave us?' Daye replied thoughtfully.

'Yes.'

'He was called Mister Meadows.'

'Monday morning, I want you interviewing this Mister Meadows.' James commanded. 'And don't come back to Templegate until you know everything about Anne-Marie De Wynter.'

Daye gave a slight smile at James' instructions. She fully agreed with them.

James drove slowly off the car park unaware that Anne-Marie was watching them leave. He was also unaware that she had a phone to her left ear.

'The Police have been here looking for you.' She said softly into the mouthpiece. 'Do not go home. In fact, it would be better for you if you just disappeared for a while.'

CHAPTER
SIXTEEN

Saturday morning arrived with a bright sun shining and a cold breeze blowing; there was also no sign of Jimmy MacGregor. His wife had stated the night before that he had indeed been ill on the Thursday but had left for work as normal on the Friday. Yet he had not been at work and had not returned home as he should have done in the evening.

When James and Daye saw Susan again early on Saturday morning Jimmy's wife was looking both perplexed and distressed. She had, understandably, demanded to know from the two officers why the Police should be interested in her husband. James had evaded her question with an 'it's a lead that we are following up on in a case that we are investigating.' James had then refused to elaborate further.

James had, however, issued a name and description to all police officers in the Bellingham area to keep a lookout for Jimmy MacGregor and to inform Detective Inspector Buchan immediately if he should be sighted. As James drove his Mondeo onto the small car park of Whittingham Computer Systems, Daye was talking on her mobile to the control room at Templegate.

As she ended her call, she turned to face James.

'There's still no sign of MacGregor.' She said thoughtfully. 'He seems to have gone to ground.'

'It's almost as though someone had tipped him off.' James replied, looking knowingly at Daye. Daye smiled back her acknowledgement of the remark which had not required an answer.

Inside the compact and tidy industrial unit that served as the HQ of Whittingham Computer Systems, James and Daye were met by a large, jovial man with a bushy black beard which had only a few grey hairs on display. James guessed his age as about mid-forties.

'I'm John Tomlinson,' the big man said with an engaging smile as he held out his hand towards James who shook it firmly. 'I believe you wanted to see me?'

'I'm detective Inspector Buchan.' James said politely showing his identification to John. 'And this,' indicating Daye, who was also showing her identification, 'is Detective Sergeant Durham.'

'I'm pleased to meet you both.' He said cordially. 'And how can I help you?'

'We are very interested in your A.V.I.S. program.' James began. 'We think someone may be using it illegally.'

John looked shocked. He still looked shocked as he led the two officers into a back office that he called the company's 'Inner Sanctum'. This office was really a portable bubble with an only access through a coded keypad door. Inside were two desks, several filing cabinets, numerous wires and cables that disappeared into the walls, and a computer bank against the right-hand wall. But on the desk in the centre was a single computer terminal, its screen displaying a pale blue coloured background while the letters were black inside pale yellow boxes with black edges. A man was sat working at the terminal, his back to the door. He rose and turned to face the three arrivals as they entered the bubble.

'This is Qasim Patel.' John introduced the young man of Asian extraction to the two officers. 'He's part of the triumvirate that runs A.V.I.S.'

'A triumvirate runs A.V.I.S.?' James queried. 'Then shouldn't there be three of you?'

John and Qasim exchanged knowing smiles.

'There are normally three of us.' Qasim began to explain, still smiling. 'But unfortunately, Nigel's new hobby prevents him from being here.'

'I think I'd better explain more fully.' John interjected. 'Nigel is our third member but is currently in hospital because he has decided to take up mountain climbing as a hobby.'

'But he isn't very good.' The ever-smiling Qasim added. 'He's so far attempted to climb three mountains and broken a limb at each attempt. It was his leg this time.'

'He likes the mountains,' James offered, 'but they don't like him.'

John and Qasim smiled at the remark.

'That's very well put.' John agreed.

'But does he still have access to A.V.I.S.?' James said more sternly as he tried to return the conversation to the reason for his and Daye's visit.

'Our passwords have to be changed every ten days.' Qasim volunteered the information, the smile having slowly left his face, 'if not. We will have no access to the system.'

'Can anyone else take over the access from him?' Daye asked quietly.

'No.' John replied firmly. 'Only each man knows his own password.' but added sharply. 'And we never share them.'

'Just what sort of access to A.V.I.S. do you have?'

'Everything,' John answered firmly patting the computer terminal softly as though he was patting a child's head, 'and from here.'

John went on to explain that only the three members of the triumvirate could enter all areas of the A.V.I.S. program, including those areas only used by each garage, and alter the information there if necessary.

'Was there some area of A.V.I.S. that was of concern to you?' John suddenly asked James. 'You said that it was being used illegally.'

'I was at Tattersall's of Brymington recently and I asked the salesman about a vehicle that he didn't have.' James explained teasingly, 'so he went onto a search screen and entered details of the vehicle that I was looking for.'

John immediately sat down at the terminal and pressed a few keys which brought up the search screen which James immediately recognised.

'That's it,' James said firmly whilst looking over John's shoulder. 'That screen can apparently search through all the inventory databases of all the garages.'

'That's correct.' John agreed. 'And if it finds a match it can request a transfer of the vehicle for you.'

'What if there isn't a match?' Daye asked quietly. 'What happens to the search information that you've put onto the screen?'

John pressed a few keys until another screen appeared in front of him.

'This is called the request screen.' John said. 'Any vehicle that a garage still requires keeps the details on this screen which all the other garages can see. And if a vehicle comes into their garage that matches the details of the wanted vehicle, they simply contact the garage making the request.'

James scratched his chin as a thought crossed his mind. 'Could a garage search another garage's records to look for a particular vehicle?'

'You mean search its archives?' John asked in puzzlement. 'Why on earth would anyone want to do that?'

'Is it possible?' James persisted forcefully.

'No, it isn't.' John insisted. 'Once a transaction is complete, the information on that transaction goes into the archive and can only be accessed by that garage.'

'Plus, the triumvirate of course,' Qasim added quickly.

'Of course,' John responded with a trace of irritation in his voice. 'But then again; why would we want to?'

'Could you access the archives of Tattersall's of Brymington?'

'Of course,' John answered, 'but why would I want to?'

'To assist us in our investigation, it could be important.'

John shrugged his shoulders as though he had not understood the remark but did as he was told anyway. Tattersall's archive suddenly filled the screen. John asked, 'What am I looking for?'

'When was the last sale of a green Range Rover?'

John entered the details and then pressed the enter key. Almost immediately the sales details of the last green Range Rover sold at Tattersall's came jumping onto the screen.

'Caroline Bamber.' James said firmly, pointing at the new owner's name. 'And one of the uses that the vehicle will be put to is doing the school run.'

'Which suggests that Caroline Bamber has probably got a child?' Daye added forcefully.

'Not only that.' James commented as he looked intently at the screen. 'These personal details of the buyer also say she is divorced, which means that she will be driving the Range Rover to the school. No husband to complicate matters.'

'Excuse me, Inspector.' John was interrupting and looking confused. 'I don't quite understand. What's this Caroline Bamber got to do with anything?'

'She was the last victim of the Balaclava Man.' James said firmly. 'And you've just shown us the way he has been finding his victims.'

'Oh My God!' John suddenly blurted out. He had obviously heard of the Balaclava Man. 'He's somehow been accessing the A.V.I.S. program?'

'No doubt about it.' James confirmed. 'The question now is 'has he also been using the A.V.I.S. program to dispose of the Range Rover?'

'You mean through the request screen?' John asked sheepishly but added quietly. 'When did the Balaclava Man steal this Range Rover?'

'It was stolen just last Tuesday.' James replied and then stood watching John as he typed the information into the A.V.I.S. program.

'This is the archive for the request screen.' John explained as the archive appeared on screen. 'We keep such information for about two years and then delete it.' John suddenly went white as he looked at the archive for last Tuesday.

'Who are Penly's of Norwich?' James demanded to know as he looked over John's shoulder and saw that this garage was the only one asking for a green Range Rover.

John hit another key to bring up the information on Penly's request for a green Range Rover.

'The request has been satisfied.' John said slowly, adding ominously. 'The vehicle was delivered yesterday and bought by the customer yesterday evening.'

'Which garage supplied the Range Rover?' James demanded firmly to know.

'It was Tattersall's of Brymington.' John said quietly, almost inaudibly. John was clearly going into shock. 'I can't believe that the Balaclava Man is using our program.'

'The balaclava Man is obviously going to want to be paid for the Range Rover.' Daye asked quietly, not wanting to shock John any further than he already was. 'How would Penly's pay for this vehicle?'

John did not answer. He just stared blankly at the screen.

'The invoice for the vehicle is sent at the same time as the vehicle.' It was Qasim who answered Daye.

'Was it by the A.V.I.S. program?' Daye asked, looking directly at Qasim who nodded his answer of 'yes'.

'But wouldn't the payment go to Tattersall's?' It was James who asked the question. 'And not the Balaclava Man'

'Yes of course.' Qasim replied thoughtfully. 'But as it is all done electronically, the Balaclava Man could be intercepting the payment somewhere on the line.'

James looked thoughtfully at John as he continued to look blankly at the computer screen.

'Are you alright, sir?' he asked John quietly to not alarm him.

John slowly nodded his head.

'I've worked for eight years on the A.V.I.S. program.' he said quietly, his voice betraying his sadness at what he had just learned. 'And to think that someone like the Balaclava Man has broken into it and was using it to steal cars and attack women is absolutely heart-breaking.'

'I can well understand how you are feeling, sir.' James responded with some well-chosen words. 'But I think that you and Qasim can finally bring this man to justice.'

John's eyes opened wide as he turned to face James.

'You mean me and Qasim?' John asked incredulously, 'how?'

'Through A.V.I.S.' Qasim suddenly said firmly as he realised James' meaning. 'We put the program together, so we are the people to find out how the Balaclava Man has been using it.'

'If all goes well,' James said hopefully, 'you'll be able to follow his trail right back to his lair.' He then added ominously. 'But it's important that you don't change anything on the A.V.I.S. program. If he sees any changes, it might alert him that we are on to him.'

Both John and Qasim smiled as they nodded their understanding; John especially had a steely look in his eyes. He clearly wanted the Balaclava Man caught.

As James and Daye exited the industrial unit of Whittingham Computer Systems the sun was shining brightly onto the throng of blue and white clad people heading towards the football ground. Some of them wore blue and white halved shirts while some youngsters even had the blue and white halves painted on their faces as a mark of their support for Blackburn Rovers, the local football team that were playing at home today.

James smiled at the good-natured supporters.

'What do we do now Sir?'

Daye's words caught James' attention and he turned towards her.

'I'm going to keep in contact here.' James began firmly but added just as firmly. 'I want you at Templegate in charge of finding Jimmy MacGregor. He's got to be somewhere.' James then put his hand into his pocket and withdrew his car keys which he threw to Daye. 'Whatever you do.' he said with a slight grin on his face. 'Don't scratch the paintwork.'

Daye looked at the battered Mondeo and from the look on her face she was obviously wondering what part of the car was available to scratch.

CHAPTER
SEVENTEEN

★ ★ ★ ★

Daye looked out of the staff room window of Red Hills High School which overlooked the staff and visitor's car park. Beyond were the trees and sprawling fields of the country park which showed the occasional red through the lush green of the grass.

A shrill bell sounded the end of the first period of lessons for that Monday morning. As the noise of the students increased along the corridors, the staff room door opened to admit a short middle-aged man wearing an ill-fitting brown suit.

'D.S. Durham?' The man asked in a husky voice as he held his hand out to shake Daye's hand. "I'm Mister Meadows. I was certainly surprised when I got your phone call this morning.'

'Thank you for seeing me, Mister Meadows.' Daye replied courteously, shaking Mr. Meadows outstretched hand while her other hand held her identification for Mr. Meadows to see. 'I was hoping you would be able to tell me about a former pupil of yours, Ann Walker?'

Mister Meadows' weather-beaten face suddenly reacted awkwardly to the name. He clearly remembered Ann Walker.

'Oh dear,' he said sorrowfully, obviously invoking bad memories. 'What's she done now?'

Daye smiled as she sat down in the chair that Mister Meadows was offering her to take whilst he sat opposite on the edge of a settee.

'I've been hearing things about her.' Daye began seriously. 'And I need to know what she was like at school.'

Mister Meadows did not immediately answer but sat on the settee with a resigned look on his face.

'What's she done?' he asked coldly as though fearing this question ever since she left Red Hills.

'I can't tell you I'm afraid.' Daye answered politely. 'I'm involved in an investigation and Ann Walker's name has cropped up.'

'I understand.' Mister meadows conceded. 'What is it that you want to know about her?'

'I need to know about her relationships with the other pupils at the school,' She began quietly, but added firmly, 'especially her relationships with the boys.'

'You mean boys such as Joshua Anderson, don't you?' Mister Meadows remarked knowingly.

Daye nodded her head slightly.

'I know just the person you need to talk to.'

Mister Meadows then stood up and hurriedly left the staff room leaving Daye looking a little puzzled as to whom he would return with. She did not have long to wait. He re-entered a few minutes later followed by a young woman in her early twenties wearing a stylish blue and green trouser suit. Daye smiled as she recognised her immediately. She had been the teacher with the schoolboys on the lawn near the school gates.

'This is Marie Shepherd.' Mister Meadows said in way of introduction to Daye. 'She was friends with Ann Walker at the time in question.'

Daye and Marie warmly shook hands as Mister Meadows said a quick 'I'll leave you to it' before exiting the staff room.

'He didn't have to leave.' Daye said in a surprised manner. 'I would have had questions for you both.'

'He had to leave.' Marie answered quietly, pointing to the chair behind Daye and indicating that she should retake her seat while she herself sat down on the settee. 'If I am to tell the truth then Mister Meadows can't be present.' She continued in a mysterious tone. She then added quickly, 'Well not without a great deal of embarrassment for me.'

'There are things you don't want him to hear?'

'Exactly,' Marie said cautiously, 'you are here because of the games Ann used to play with the boys, aren't you?'

'Yes I am.' Daye replied firmly. 'I believe she used to make them do things out of character.'

Marie nodded her head slowly as though she was ashamed of herself. She slowly pushed her long brunette hair away from her face as she suddenly sat upright and faced Daye.

'Ann used to have a theory that you could get anyone to do whatever you wanted by making them believe whatever you told them,' Marie said firmly, adding angrily, 'even if it was a pack of lies.'

'And the boys just believed her?'

'Of course, they did.' Marie replied quietly, 'because she always sweetened the lies with a promise to give them something if they would do something for her.' She gave out a feeble laugh as she recounted the sweeteners for Daye. 'I'll give you a kiss; you can have a feel; I'll go to bed with you. And the boys at this point would feel sorry for Ann and do whatever she wanted. They were putty in her hands.'

'You went along with this?' queried Daye.

'At first,' Marie answered sombrely. 'It was a joke, and nobody got hurt,' but she then added thoughtfully. 'And then the situation got more serious which led to boys being expelled.'

'The teachers found out?'

'They found out everything.' Marie replied. 'A carefully timed anonymous phone call, a boy expelled; a future ruined.'

'Just like Joshua Anderson.' Daye probed to test Marie's response. 'Who made the phone call do you think?'

'How many guesses do you want?' Marie challenged. 'It was Ann of course. It was Ann every time.'

'How do you know this?' Daye asked quizzically.

'Because I was Ann's best friend at the time,' Marie answered coldly. 'She used to tell me everything.'

'But when boys were being expelled,' Daye asked firmly, 'why did you not come forward and tell someone?'

'It was too late.' Marie answered weakly, looking like a lost child as she stared blankly at the floor. She suddenly sat bolt upright and stared directly at Daye. 'I'd already been asked by Mister Meadows 'did I know what was going on?''

'And what did you reply?'

Marie smiled lamely. 'I denied knowing anything about it.' She stared blankly again at the floor before looking again at Daye. 'I denied knowing anything every time Mister Meadows asked me.'

'It sounds like he didn't believe you the first time you denied knowing anything.'

'Of course, he didn't believe me.' Marie almost spat the words. 'But what could I do? I couldn't very well suddenly say that I knew something after all, could I? I would end up looking completely stupid and embarrassed.'

'What does Mister Meadows think now?' Daye pointedly asked.

'Why do you think he left the room?' Marie replied knowingly.

Daye smiled to herself; Marie was obviously in an awkward situation. Mister Meadows clearly knew the truth.

'But what really frightened me was a conversation that I had with Ann just before our final exams.' Marie continued nervously and quietly, her fingers fidgeting with a handkerchief that she held. 'She talked about dominating boys and wondered how far she could go.' She dabbed away a tear from the corner of her eye with the plain white handkerchief. 'She wondered could she actually get a boy to kill for her.'

Chairs and tables flew viciously across the room before twisting into awkward shapes of metal as they collided with the plain white walls of the cell. Two burly white dressed orderlies closed in quickly on the angry young man who was about to hurl another chair at them. As they struggled to pin him to the floor a female nurse, dressed in white like the orderlies, injected the young man with a syringe full of sedative.

'I'm afraid this is happening most days' now.' the doctor said sombrely as he looked through the tiny window into the cell. 'All we have to do is to mention the name 'Anne-Marie' to him and he literally goes berserk.'

James Buchan looked impassively through the window at the drowsy Benny Gordon who was lying helpless and restrained on the cell floor.

'What on earth has caused this?' he asked.

'That's a good question.' The doctor quietly replied, his middle-aged face betraying his obvious concern for his patient. 'He's keeping something bottled up inside him. He wants to tell us what it is but is afraid to tell us because of this Anne-Marie.'

'Is he afraid of her?' James asked quizzically.

'I don't think it is fear,' The doctor replied thoughtfully, 'but she certainly has some sort of hold over him, and that is what is eating him up inside.'

CHAPTER
EIGHTEEN

★ ★ ★ ★

Upstairs in James Buchan's office, James was sat at his desk as he briefed Daye on Benny Gordon's condition.

'He's the only one that can confirm what Marie Shepherd told me this morning.' Daye said downheartedly. James nodded his head in agreement having just previously heard Daye's report on her visit to Red Hills High School, 'unless Anne-Marie decides to confess of course.' She added hopefully but her tone of voice lacked any hope at all.

James smiled at Daye but did not answer her. He did not need to.

'We may struggle to get a confession out of her.' He suddenly spoke in a mysterious tone, 'but she doesn't know what we know.'

Daye looked quizzically at her superior officer.

'She doesn't know that you have spoken to her former best friend this morning.' James explained knowingly. And then added quickly, 'Nor does she know that Benny Gordon is unlikely to talk to us at all.'

It was now Daye's turn to nod knowingly. She fully understood what James was saying.

James's mobile phone which was lying on his desk suddenly rang out. James picked it up and looked at the number.

'It's Ferguson.' He said sounding a little surprised. He put the phone to the side of his face and spoke into the mouthpiece. 'Yes Ferguson?'

James looked pleased as he listened to Ferguson and hurriedly grabbed a pencil and notepad to scribble down something. He finished the conversation by saying 'Thank you, Ferguson. I owe you one.'

'He's discovered something good?' Daye asked hopefully

'Only the manufacturer of the 'Balaclava Man's' tracksuit,' James said excitedly as he replaced the phone on his desk. 'And this....' he said holding up the notepad that he had just written on, 'is the name of the one and only local distributor of that company's products.' James held his breath teasingly. 'And it is in Blackburn.'

The office door opened quietly as the desk sergeant entered.

'That MacGregor fellow that you were looking for,' he spoke firmly but softly as he looked directly at James. 'He's just walked into reception with another man. I've put them in the interview room.'

Jimmy MacGregor looked forlorn and frightened as he sat in the interview room in Templegate Police Station.

'You're doing the right thing, Jimmy.' The elderly man sitting next to Jimmy said reassuringly.

Jimmy was not so sure. But after hiding out in a broken down and unused allotment shed for two days, he had concluded that hiding like that was not going to help him.

But what was he to do? And what was he hiding from? He had not actually done anything wrong. He was just following Anne-Marie's advice. But he didn't know why.

The interview room door opened with a flourish as first James, quickly followed by Daye, entered the room and silently sat down opposite the two men. Daye switched the tape recorder, set into the wall at the end of the table, on.

'I'm D.I. Buchan,' James said firmly into the tape's microphone.

'I'm D.S Durham,' Daye said just as firmly as her superior officer.

'If you could just say your names for the benefit of the tape, please,' James said to the two men, indicating the microphone.

Both men looked anxiously at each other before the older man told Jimmy to speak.

'Jimmy MacGregor.' The younger man mumbled.

The older man next to Jimmy then lent forward to get his mouth close to the microphone before speaking in a forceful and authoritative voice.

'I'm Richard Ashcroft'. He began, looking directly into James Buchan's eyes. 'I'm the Managing Director of Ashcroft's Fabrications and Jimmy's father-in-law. And I would like to know what all this is about.'

'What this is all about, Mister Ashcroft.' James said in a firm and strong voice. 'Is that we are conducting a murder enquiry.'

'Murder?!' Ashcroft interrupted with alarming incredulity. 'What are you talking about? Who's been murdered?'

'Jack Manning.' James replied forcibly. 'Someone that Jimmy knows a lot about'

Ashcroft turned wide eyed and open mouthed towards Jimmy who was looking down at the tabletop looking sheepish and dejected.

'What's he talking about Jimmy?' Ashcroft demanded to know.

'If I could ask the questions, please Mister Ashcroft.?' It was James' turn to interrupt Ashcroft. James then turned to face the younger man. 'Benny Gordon has confessed to the murder.'

'Well, if you have the man....' Ashcroft started to interrupt again.

'Please, Mister Ashcroft.' This time it was Daye cutting him short using a very determined and forceful tone of voice. 'These are questions for Mister MacGregor to answer.'

Ashcroft was about to speak again but then thought better of it.

'Did you know that Benny had confessed?' James spoke directly to Jimmy who replied with a shake of his head.

'Please speak for the benefit of the tape, Mister MacGregor.' Daye demanded courteously.

'I don't know anything about either Benny or Jack Manning.' Jimmy stumbled with the words and could not look up from the table.

'But you must know something Jimmy.' James insisted 'Otherwise why have you been hiding from us? And by the way,' He added quickly. 'Where have you been hiding?'

Jimmy did not answer immediately. He sat stony faced looking crestfallen at the tabletop. He only reacted when Richard sharply told him to 'Answer the question'.

Jimmy looked first at Richard before turning towards James.

'I've been sleeping in a disused Allotment shed.' He said softly

'Why were you hiding from us?' James persisted, adding menacingly, 'And what are you trying to withhold from us?'

Jimmy looked shaken and afraid.

'Benny didn't know anything about Jack Manning,' James continued firmly. 'So, someone must have told him about him. Was that someone you?'

Jimmy bit his lip as though struggling to find the right words to say.

Suddenly he blurted out, 'I haven't mentioned anything to Benny.' Jimmy was almost crying as he spoke. 'I don't even know this Jack Manning so how could I tell him anything?'

'Perhaps your girlfriend told you all about him?'

Richard looked startled by James' question. He did not say anything though but turned angrily towards his son-in-law who cowed away from him.

'I take it you don't know about Jimmy's girlfriend, Mr Ashcroft?'

Richard's face turned red with anger as he glared at Jimmy.

Suddenly he turned to face James. 'No, I did not.' He said with Fury before turning again to Jimmy. 'Who is the little slut?' He demanded to know.

'I haven't got a girlfriend. 'Jimmy shouted, throwing his hands into the air for added effect. 'I don't know anything about this. I don't know Jack Manning and I'm not having an affair with anyone. I love only Susan.'

Richard did not respond but he did not look convinced either.

'You used to meet her at your allotment, Jimmy.' James said quietly before adding more forcefully, 'the same allotment that Benny worked on.'

'I don't know what you're talking about' Jimmy shouted, his wild eyes scanning the room as though trying to find a way out.

'Who is this slut?' Richard demanded to know, his eyes looking penetratingly at James. 'Do I know her?'

'Oh, I think you do.' James replied softly. 'She's called Anne-Marie De Wynter.'

'My P.A. was his girlfriend!?' Richard almost screamed in surprise, his eyes glaring daggers at his son-in-law.

'She happens to be Jack Manning's niece.'

Jimmy looked pleadingly at his Father-in-law and though his mouth opened and shut again, no words came out.

'I came with you because I thought I could help you.' Richard was clearly struggling to control his temper as he spoke. 'You had better start telling the truth my lad........'

'I haven't got a girlfriend!!!' Jimmy screamed at his father-in-law. 'I've got nothing to do with this murder.'

'I'm washing my hands of my son-in-law.' Richard exploded angrily as he jumped up from his seat. Turning to look straight into James' eyes he added vehemently, 'do with him what you will.'

With a final look of contempt at Jimmy, Richard stormed out of the interview room.

'Interview suspended.' James said softly to the tape, but to Jimmy he said. 'I think you need to realise the situation you're in is serious.'

With that, James and Daye got up to leave the room leaving a stunned and confused Jimmy alone with his thoughts and a Police Officer standing next to the door.

Outside in the corridor, James and Daye quickened their pace to catch up with Richard Ashcroft.

'Could I just have a quick word with you, Mister Ashcroft?'

Richard stopped and turned to face James, but his blood shot eyes, and reddened cheeks showed that he was still fuming at his son-in-law.

CHAPTER
NINETEEN

Daye walked briskly along the pedestrian walkway between two rows of shops on King William Street. She mingled with the shoppers as they browsed the window displays or sat chatting to friends on the varnished benches that lined the walkway. She eventually stopped outside a sports shop named 'Blackburn Sports Emporium'.

Withdrawing the piece of paper from her pocket that James had given her after showing Richard Ashcroft into an office, Daye confirmed that she was at the correct address that Ferguson had given him. She also pulled out a small plastic bag that contained the chewed remains of a piece of blue cloth that had been retrieved from Sosabowski's mouth.

Once inside the shop she looked around the various displays ranging from sports equipment to footwear. It was while she was examining a display of badminton rackets that a young female sales assistant approached her and asked her 'do you need any assistance madam?'

Daye produced her I.D. and said to the assistant that she wanted to see the manager.

'What can I do for you?' the manager, a tall thin thirty something with dyed hair trying to make himself look twenty something, said to Daye as she walked into his office and held out her I.D. towards him. She noticed from his lapel badge that he was called Greg Hammond.

The female shop assistant quietly closed the office door behind her as she left just as the manager asked Daye to sit down on a hard backed chair opposite his plain wood and plastic desk. He then sat down on a chrome chair which clearly did not go with the desk although it certainly looked more comfortable than the chair that Daye was sat on.

'I understand that your shop is the sole distributor of Lysander Sportswear products in this area.' Daye began quietly, adding quickly, 'especially tracksuits.'

'That's correct. We are.' Greg replied politely, adjusting the way he sat in his chair; nervously thought Daye. 'Can I ask what this is about?'

Daye handed over the plastic bag containing the torn piece of blue fabric to the manager who partly closed his eyes as he focused on it.

'Where on earth has this been?' he asked quizzically.

'It got chewed up by a German shepherd.' Daye replied. 'But it has been identified as a Lysander product.'

'Well. I recognise the colour.' He said positively, inspecting the piece of fabric very carefully. 'It is from a range of tracksuit that we used to stock from them.'

'You used to?' Daye asked.

'It wasn't a good seller.' Greg remarked apologetically, as though he blamed himself for the low sales. 'We had to return the remaining stocks to Lysander.'

'But you did sell some?' Daye asked hopefully.

'Only a handful I'm afraid.' Greg replied in a low voice, before adding quickly. 'What is this about?'

'Did you sell any tracksuits with matching blue balaclavas?' Daye asked firmly, ignoring Greg's question.

Greg sat bolt upright at Daye's question; his eyes wide open as he looked directly into her brown eyes.

'This isn't about the 'balaclava man' is it?' He said in a voice so quiet it sounded like he did not want to say the name.

'You must keep this conversation confidential, Mister Hammond.' Daye ordered firmly. 'This is a dangerous man that we are after, and we obviously don't want him to be forewarned.'

'Of course,' Greg replied, raising his arms to emphasize his understanding of Daye's order. 'I've read about him in the paper. Do you think.......?'

'Please just answer my question, Mister Hammond.' Daye interrupted sternly. 'Did you sell any of those tracksuits with matching blue balaclavas?'

Greg thought carefully before answering. 'I'm not sure.' He said defensibly. 'But I could check my records for you if you like.'

Daye said, 'That would be very helpful,' and got up to follow Greg out of the office.

Richard Ashcroft was very agitated and red faced as he sat beside the plain wooden desk in the Spartan looking office that looked more like a storeroom than an operational office.

James entered the office carrying two cups of tea and offered one cup to Richard.

'Sorry about the mess in here,' James said apologetically, looking at some half-opened cartons that lay untidily on one side of the room. 'This room is only ever used in an emergency.'

Richard took hold of the offered cup of tea and smiled half-heartedly at James.

'So,' he began dryly. 'My son-in-law is an emergency now, is he?'

'It is rather urgent that we discover what is going on.' James replied solemnly, 'especially with regard to the murder of Jack Manning by Benny Gordon.'

'I'm not sure that I can help you there.' Richard replied quietly as he took a sip of tea before continuing. 'I don't know either name.'

'But your son-in-law does.' James said firmly, adding quickly, 'And so does your P.A.'

'Has he really been having an affair with her?' Richard asked angrily, and by the tone of his voice he already knew the answer. James did not answer but slightly nodded his head. 'What a stupid bloody fool!' Richard screamed. 'Will he never learn?'

'I take it that he has had other affairs?' James probed firmly but politely.

'Of course, he has.' Richard replied bitterly. 'And Susan has been silly enough to take him back each time. This holiday in Tunisia was a final warning to Jimmy. And what has he done with it?'

'Will Susan still take him back again?'

Richard shrugged his shoulders in despair and heaved a deep sigh of forlorn hope.

'What has Jimmy's behaviour been like since he came back from Tunisia?'

Richard did not answer James' question immediately. He sat with a thoughtful expression on his face as though pondering on what answer he should give.

'I picked them up from the airport when they arrived back.' He slowly and carefully answered. 'Everything seemed fine. In fact, they both seemed quite happy.'

'Then what happened?'

Richard smiled before answering. 'Jimmy made a phone call that night.' Richard said quietly. 'I don't know who it was too, but the conversation must have unnerved him. Susan said his face was snow white when he put the phone down. She asked him what was wrong, but he wouldn't answer...........He never answered her. Nor me when I queried that phone call.'

'That phone call was probably to Benny Gordon's mother.' James explained. 'She'd just told him that Benny had been arrested.'

'I don't like the sound of that.' Richard said solemnly. 'That shouldn't have unnerved him unless.......'

Richard suddenly stopped talking.

James already knew what the ending was: '.......he was involved.'

'Have you ever heard of a Jessica Morris?' James suddenly asked firmly.

'No.' Richard quickly replied, with an astonished look on his face. 'Why?'

'Last Wednesday your son-in-law was overheard making threats against her.' James said firmly. 'And on Thursday he spent a lot of time trying to locate her.' He then added with a steely hardness in his voice. 'And no one has seen her since.'

Richard looked shocked as he stared straight into James' eyes. He clearly wanted to say something but found himself completely dumbfounded.

'We need to know what Jimmy was doing on those two days.' James demanded forcefully.

'There's nothing more I can tell you.' Richard said weakly, his eyes turned towards the floor.

Greg Hammond was sat behind a plain wooden desk looking at a computer screen.

'This contains all our stock records.' He said slowly as he scrolled through each screen. 'It may take some time to find the records that we want.'

'Take your time, Mister Hammond.' Daye replied politely, with an underlying tone of authority. 'We must get this right.'

Greg slowly and methodically inspected the stock records whilst Daye looked around the stockroom office. It was a plastic bubble containing a table, two chairs and a computer keyboard and screen which was on its own desk next to the table. Outside in the stockroom was a dishevelled collection of cartons and boxes, some of which had been opened and partially emptied.

'Here it is.' Greg suddenly exclaimed, pointing excitedly at an entry on the computer screen.' And it's the only sale of a tracksuit and balaclava sold to the same buyer.'

Daye looked at the copy of the sales slip complete with the name and credit card details of the purchaser,

'Print that off for me please, would you?' Daye asked, struggling to contain her own excitement. This was the breakthrough that she had been looking for.

CHAPTER
TWENTY

★ ★ ★ ★

James was smiling as he re-entered the interview room where Jimmy MacGregor sat looking forlorn with his head down on his chest and his eyes fixed onto the tabletop. He replaced the mobile phone back into his pocket after he had just completed a short phone conversation with Daye. He was pleased with the outcome of her visit to the Blackburn Sports Emporium. He was hoping to be just as pleased with the outcome of this interview with Jimmy MacGregor.

'That was a very interesting chat with your father-in-law.' James said confidently as he took his seat opposite Jimmy. 'And I've got a feeling that he might be looking for a new P.A.'

'I'm not having an affair with Anne-Marie!' Jimmy shouted angrily.

'That's not our information, Jimmy.' James replied forcefully with a steely tone in his voice.

'Then your information is wrong.' Jimmy shouted again although the direction of his eyes fell towards the floor.

'Let's try a different question.' James said quietly, hoping to catch Jimmy off guard. 'Why did you make threats against Jessica Morris last Wednesday in the office of Mister Ashcroft's P.A.?' adding accusingly, 'a woman who you claim is not your girlfriend.'

'I don't know any Jessica Morris.' Jimmy cried out loud, his voice now like a whimpering dog.

'She's the cousin of Benny Gordon.' James said firmly, adding sharply, 'And she has been to the allotment and spoken directly to you.' James' voice fell silent for a moment before adding firmly. 'I believe she was threatening to tell your wife about your affair with Anne-Marie De Wynter.'

Jimmy sat bolt upright and looked directly into James' eyes. His mouth opened slightly but he said nothing.

That one has shaken him to the core, James thought to himself. *Now he has got something to think about.*

'I want to see a solicitor.' Jimmy suddenly demanded, his eyes looking wild and confused.

James looked at the name on the printout that Daye had just handed him.

'Pamela Frankland.' He said softly, raising his right eyebrow to indicate that the name was unknown to him. 'Do we have anything on her?'

'Nothing at all I'm afraid.' Daye replied as she sat down at her desk and shuffled some papers that were lying in front of her. She picked one up and looked at it. 'This one from C.R.O. shows she has no criminal record at all,' adding with a smile, 'not even a parking ticket.'

'A goody two shoes, eh?' James said sarcastically. 'Better have a background check on her anyway.'

'I've got a P.C. from behind the front desk doing that now.' Daye replied with a smile.

'Good.' James commented. 'When you've got all the information together, we'll go and see her. In the meantime, we've got Mister MacGregor to sort out. He's denying absolutely everything.' James went and sat down behind his desk before continuing. 'He's denying having any sort of relationship with Anne-Marie De Wynter and has never heard of or spoken to Jessica Morris.'

'What's he playing at?' gasped Daye.

'I think he's made some sort of arrangement with Anne-Marie where they both deny any sort of relationship with each other.' James said solemnly. 'He obviously doesn't know that she isn't keeping to the arrangement.'

'Going on what I've heard about her this morning I think Anne-Marie could be setting Jimmy up for a fall.' Daye said solemnly, adding thoughtfully. 'Just like I think she has set up Benny Gordon'

James looked with intrigue at his D.S., his blue green eyes imploring her to continue.

'We know that Anne-Marie knows Benny.' Daye began firmly, flaring her nostrils as she spoke. 'They'd met at Jimmy's allotment. A woman matching Anne-Marie's description has visited Benny at his home.'

'But that description from the neighbour was rather vague.' James interrupted forcefully. 'It could have applied to just about anyone. Maybe it was Anne-Marie; but then again, maybe it wasn't.'

'I accept that.' Daye conceded. 'The point is that the description could have been Anne-Marie, a person known to Benny.'

'True.' James agreed.

'But on top of that,' Daye continued, her tone of voice lowering mysteriously which immediately caught James' attention. 'The way that we were led to Jimmy's allotment was through an anonymous phone call; A method that Anne-Marie used to use at Red Hills to betray the boys.'

James rubbed his chin thoughtfully before speaking.

'So, Jimmy may not have been directly involved in Jack Manning's murder?'

'He's not totally excluded, Sir.' Daye offered politely, 'but, personally, I think Anne-Marie was more directly involved than Jimmy.'

'She certainly had something to gain from Manning's death.' James said quietly but with conviction. 'That coin collection for a start. But what would Jimmy gain?'

'All three met at his allotment shed.' Daye said firmly. 'Surely he must have known what was going on.' Daye then added quickly. 'And if Anne-Marie was setting him up, wouldn't she have told Jimmy all about her uncle?'

James did not reply to his sergeant's question but slowly nodded his head in agreement. He sat looking out the window with a thoughtful gaze on his face. Suddenly he turned around and faced Daye.

'Was Anne-Marie involved with Jessica's disappearance?' He asked firmly with a determined look on his face, 'because of what we know now Jimmy must have been. He was overheard making threats against Jessica and spent all day Thursday trying to find her.'

'Had she anything to gain from her disappearance?' Daye queried in a doubtful manner as though she disbelieved that Anne-Marie could have been involved. 'Jimmy was on the point of losing everything.' adding with greater emphasis, 'and probably already has.'

'Would you get into a taxi wearing dirty and scruffy looking shoes?' James asked quietly and carefully.

'Where did that come from?'

Daye almost laughed when she heard James' question but then a more serious expression took hold of her as though a stroke of realisation had overwhelmed her.

'Anne-Marie was at the Black Bull on Wednesday night.' She said thoughtfully. 'Aled said she had walked there.'

'But she told us she had gone to the Black Bull in a taxi.' James added firmly. 'So how did she mess up her shoes?'

'You were wondering once had Anne-Marie and Jessica met up on that Wednesday night.'

'Yes, I did.' James answered thoughtfully. 'But we've got no actual evidence that they did meet.'

'But Wednesday night was the last time that Jessica was seen alive.' Daye pointed out forcefully.

'By her Aunt Julie as she left to go home.' James added firmly and nodding his head towards Daye. Maybe there was evidence to find after all.

CHAPTER
TWENTY-ONE

★ ★ ★ ★

James sat at his desk, coffee in hand, reading a file on a new case to be added to his ever-growing list of unsolved cases. This one concerned a masked raider, armed with a baseball bat, of corner shops who had been plaguing Bellingham shopkeepers for several weeks. He had not actually hurt anyone but had held the bat in a threatening manner as though he would not hesitate to use it. James had raised the subject of his shortage of officers with his Superintendent but had only been given vague promises of replacements based on vaguer promises of funds to pay for them. James put the file into his pending tray as he literally had no one to investigate it.

The office door opened to admit a smiling Daye Durham.

'Good morning, Sir.' Daye said in a chirpy manner as she walked towards her desk. 'After struggling all night we've finally got a solicitor for Jimmy MacGregor.' She said through her smile. 'But it isn't the one he wanted.' Daye crossed the floor and sat down behind her desk adding, 'He wanted Ben Samuels, but he declined claiming a conflict of interest.'

'What conflict?' James queried. 'And who is Ben Samuels anyway?'

'Oh, he's a genuine solicitor.' Daye explained. 'He also happens to be the legal advisor to Ashcroft Fabrications.'

James' smiled as he asked, 'Do I detect that Daddy-in-law Richard has thrown Jimmy to the wolves?'

'That's what it sounds like to me.' Daye agreed. 'Richard Ashcroft must have contacted Samuels as soon as he left Templegate yesterday. Jimmy is now talking with the duty solicitor, Roy Oxford.'

'Maybe he'll now realise that he is on his own and come back to his senses.' James said hopefully, adding menacingly 'We'll let him stew in his own juice for a while.'

Daye, still smiling, nodded her head in agreement.

The office door opened quietly to admit a burley police sergeant.

'Sorry to interrupt you, Sir.' He began politely, 'There is a Qasim Patel of Whittingham's at the front desk. He says he has something that you'll want to see. We've put him in the interview room for you.'

'Good man.' James replied quickly, rising speedily from his chair.

Nothing more was said as both James and Daye hurried out of the office and made their way quickly to the interview room.

Qasim was sat at the table with an open folder in front of him. He rose as James and Daye entered.

'Good to see you again, Sir.' Qasim said politely, withdrawing some papers from the open folder.

'Good to see you too, Qasim,' James replied just as politely before adding sharply. 'Have you got something for us?'

'We got a breakthrough last night.' Qasim said excitedly as he spread the papers on the table in front of him. He pointed to one printout that showed a black edged box containing three names in black on a yellow background. 'This is the master log,' Qasim continued, his excitement not diminished. 'Those are the names of the three people with full access to the A.V.I.S. system.'

'The Triumvirate' James confirmed looking at the names on the printout.

'Correct.' Qasim agreed, but added sombrely, 'except there are four names there.'

James looked more closely at the names before turning quizzically towards Qasim.

'Am I going blind or what?' he asked in astonishment. 'There are only three names there.'

Qasim put another printout next to the first one which contained the three names; this printout was identical to the first one except that it showed four names in the master log.

'What's going on here?' James asked in amazement. 'I recognise the first three names. But who is King Kong?'

'The Balaclava Man.' Qasim replied, suppressing a clear tone of anger in his voice. 'When he entered the name 'King Kong' into the master log he used yellow letters on a yellow background so that no one could see that the log had an extra name in it.'

'But that's a child's trick,' Daye suddenly blurted out. 'Surely you had safeguards in place to prevent this.'

'We do now.' Qasim said weakly. 'But they were put in when the system was completed and became operational.'

'Then 'King Kong' was added to the master log during development.' James said firmly.

Qasim nodded his head in acknowledgement of James' statement. He did not add anything else as his face showed both shame and apology.

'How was this 'King Kong' able to use the A.V.I.S. system?' James demanded to know.

'We were able to track his movements on the system using a built-in tracker.' Qasim explained. 'First, he would search the live request forms looking for vehicles that were wanted. Then he would search the garages archives too see if anyone had ever had a matching vehicle.'

'I thought only you could do that?' queried Daye.

'As soon as he entered his name into the master log, he was granted full access to the system.'

'So, he could request a vehicle if he wanted it?' James asked although it was partly a statement. 'And send it to another garage that wanted that vehicle?'

'Correct.' Qasim said firmly, adding 'And send an invoice to get payment as well.'

'Get payment?' James queried. 'How would that be done?'

'By electronic transfer,' Qasim replied, 'from garage to garage.'

'But surely that would mean transferring funds from one finance department to another one.' James said strongly. 'Does that mean that the Balaclava Man has got some sort of connection with a finance department?

'That's absolutely certain.'

'Which garage's finance department is he using?' James asked with some urgency.

'Tattersall's of Brymington.' Qasim said quietly. 'He even found the last victim's car, a Range Rover, in Tattersall's own archive.'

'Was anyone from Tattersall's involved with the development of the A.V.I.S. system?'

Qasim smiled and handed James a piece of A4 size paper. There were three names on it. Unfortunately, James did not recognise any of the names although he did hope that Pamela Frankland's name may have been on the list. But it was not.

'Anyone of those three could be 'King Kong'. He said decisively. 'Each one of them could have inputted the name 'King Kong' into the Master Log.' Qasim then added quickly, 'And each one is still employed there.'

James looked again at the names on the list and then said 'Thank you' to Qasim but added firmly. 'Don't make any alterations to the system that might make him suspicious. Just monitor it for now and alert us to anything that he might be doing.'

'That's already in hand, Sir.'

James smiled a pleasing smile at the young Asian man. He was very pleased with Qasim.

As they said goodbye to Qasim at the front desk, a young PC stepped out from behind a cabinet and handed Daye a folder.

'Here's the background information on Pamela Frankland that you wanted Sarge.' He said blandly, as though he was not really interested in the task that he had just done for Daye.

'When you address me, Constable, you call me Sergeant.' Daye reproached him sharply. 'Not Sarge. Remember that in future.'

'Yes, Sarge.' He stuttered but then quickly corrected himself. 'Sorry, Sergeant.'

Daye carried the folder with her but did not look at it. Instead, she entered the C.I.D. room and placed the folder on her desk. As she turned back towards the office door where James was waiting, she was anticipating the coming interview with Jimmy MacGregor.

Jimmy was sat next to his solicitor, Roy Oxford, in the interview room. Daye smiled to herself because Jimmy looked like he was lost and full of self-pity. Roy on the other hand looked like a fit mid-thirties man who had just had a good work out at the gym.

James and Daye sat opposite the two men. It was James who turned on the recording machine and waited for the two men opposite to introduce themselves which they duly did.

'I want to first say that my client is prepared to co-operate fully with your investigation.' Roy Oxford said with determination, 'and he will make a full statement afterwards.'

'Thank you, Mr. Oxford.' James replied just as firmly. He then looked at the forlorn Jimmy MacGregor and imagined what Roy Oxford had said to him

'You have said previously that you did not have a relationship with Anne-Marie De Wynter.' James said forcefully, almost threateningly. 'Can you now confirm that you did have a relationship with her?'

Jimmy lamely nodded.

'Answer for the tape please.' Daye commanded.

'Yes.' Jimmy replied weakly.

Jimmy then went on to explain the nature of his relationship with Anne-Marie. Daye looked closely at Jimmy as he spoke. He had clearly been warned by his solicitor of his situation and told, or possibly ordered, to tell the truth. Daye also wondered if Jimmy had been involved in the killing of Jack Manning, although she was still unsure as to his involvement in the disappearance of Jessica Morris.

'So, you used to meet Anne-Marie at your allotment?' James asked casually, 'how often?'

'Most weeks,' Jimmy replied nonchalantly, 'sometimes two or three times.'

'Was it the same at the Black Bear?' James suddenly asked. 'How often did you meet there?'

Jimmy looked surprised at the question but answered it anyway. 'We sometimes went for a walk in the area and finished up having a meal at the Black Bear.'

'How often was that?'

'Once a month I suppose.'

'What about last Wednesday?' James asked more forcefully.

'What about last Wednesday?' Jimmy looked totally perplexed as he asked the question, adding quickly. 'I don't think we have been to the black bear for nearly two months'

Both James and Daye smiled as they looked at the puzzled expression on Jimmy's face. His answer to the question told the Police Officers a lot more than what Jimmy realised.

At least Jimmy appeared to be co-operating with them and duly signed a statement as his solicitor had promised.

'On the basis of this statement,' Roy Oxford said with conviction. 'I would ask for bail to be given him.'

'I think we can agree to that,' James said in an amicable tone, 'providing that he has no contact with Anne-Marie De Wynter and can provide a secure address.'

James looked at Jimmy and wondered what address he was going to give.........if any.

CHAPTER
TWENTY-TWO

★ ★ ★ ★

The water in the swimming pool was cool and relaxing but smelt of an overuse of chlorine. It was early in the morning; 6:47 according to Daye's waterproof watch. She loved swimming but her workload recently had limited her chances of indulging her passion for anything aquatic. But that did not bother her if she was alone in the pool like now.

She swam on her back looking up towards the brightly coloured tiled ceiling which depicted a Victorian seaside scene. Daye closed her eyes and slowly went into a dream world which was full of peace and tranquillity. She could hear nothing, not even the swing doors of the entrance to the pool. All she could sense was a pair of eyes looking intently at her.

Daye suddenly opened her eyes and gradually beamed a broad smile at the young woman standing at the poolside.

'Hello Emily.' She called out.

Daye knew that Emily was twenty-five years old but was only four feet tall due to a condition called Achondroplasia which is a genetic disorder which results in dwarfism. But despite her size and condition Emily was very athletic and would throw herself energetically into swimming, weight training and self-defence, at which she was exceptionally good.

'Hi,' Emily replied eagerly, brushing her shoulder length blond hair away from her blue eyes as well as putting her full kit bag on the floor. 'Could I have a talk with you?'

Daye could see a serious look on Emily's face and so she hauled herself out of the pool and stood dripping in her one-piece white swimsuit beside her.

'Let me get changed,' Daye said strongly, 'and I'll meet you in the cafe.'

A few minutes later Daye was putting her kit bag down on the cafe floor next to Emily's kit bag. Emily herself was nearby placing two cups of tea on to a red plastic tabletop. She smiled at Daye as she sat on a matching plastic chair. Daye sat down opposite her.

'Going off the expression on your face you have something urgent that you want to talk to me about.' Daye said forcefully but pleasantly, 'Cut to the chase.' Daye added. 'What's your problem?'

'Don't miss much, do you?' Emily replied with a half-smile on her face. 'You know my parents own a corner shop in Bellingham?'

'Yes.' Daye answered firmly. 'On Grasmere Street, isn't it?'

'That's right.' Emily acknowledged. 'About four weeks ago the shop was raided by a masked man wielding a baseball bat.' Daye sat upright with pricked ears. She had heard of this raider and knew that he was not being investigated. Obviously, she did not disclose that to Emily. 'You can imagine the effect on my mother who was alone in the shop at the time.' Emily continued, her words becoming choked as she spoke. 'She's been a bag of nerves since and although she gave a statement to a uniformed officer at the time, we have heard nothing since.' Emily was clearly getting angry as she spoke. 'I have rung the police several times to find out what is going on. And I am just being fobbed off.' Tears of anger were welling up in her eyes, 'Quite frankly.' She suddenly shouted. 'I don't think the police are doing anything. And that is a disgrace.'

'We're rather short staffed at the moment.' Daye tried to explain.

'Don't you think that is wearing a bit thin?' Emily interrupted angrily, 'Isn't it more likely that you lot would rather stay in the canteen eating doughnuts and drinking coffee?'

Daye allowed herself a sly smile.

'I think you've seen too many American Police Shows.'

'It's not funny, Daye.' Emily shouted. 'I want something done about this.'

'Quite right too,' Daye agreed, 'I can't promise anything, but I know one person that I can talk too'

'Please.' Emily replied softly as she slowly calmed down. 'I'm sorry for sounding off.'

'Don't worry, Emily.' Daye said quietly. 'Just leave it to me.'

James Buchan was sat at his office desk. He had an open file on his desktop in front of him, but he was not looking at it. In fact, with his hands clasped together in front of him as though in prayer it looked like he was trying to communicate with the almighty. He only stirred from his contemplative posture when he looked up at the office door as it opened to allow Daye to enter.

'Good morning, Daye.' He called to his sergeant and then added quickly when he saw her wet hair. 'Been swimming with the fishes, have we?'

'I haven't been to the pool for ages.' She replied wistfully but added with a smile. 'But I certainly feel better for going.'

'We've still got Jimmy MacGregor in the cells.' James suddenly said with a serious tone in his voice.'

'I thought we were going to give him bail?' Daye queried.

'Only if he could supply a secure address,' James answered sombrely, and then quickly added. 'And nobody seems to want him. And that includes his wife.'

'That's very interesting.' Daye remarked. 'It looks like everybody has turned against him.' Daye then flared her nostrils as she thought deeply before adding. 'I wonder if he has realised that Anne-Marie is one of those people.'

James smiled at Daye's remark.

'I think we should ask him.' He said whilst still smiling.

James and Daye entered the interview room and sat opposite Jimmy MacGregor. Both officers looked a little surprised to see Jimmy sat on his own without his solicitor present.

'Are you sure............?' James began quietly but was quickly interrupted.

'No one seems to want anything to do with me.' He said, his voice full of self-pity. 'Even my own relatives have refused to give me a secure address. And yet I haven't done anything wrong.'

'Then why don't you just tell us the truth about what has been going on?' James prompted him firmly.

'One question first.' Jimmy demanded. 'What exactly has Anne-Marie been saying?'

'Now you know ......' James begun but was sharply interrupted again by Jimmy.

'Never mind that load of nonsense.' He bellowed at the Police Officer. 'We had a deal and I think she has betrayed me.'

'What makes you say that?' James asked pretending all innocence.

'I had a lot of time to think last night, and certain things do not add up.' Jimmy's voice was beginning to crack with anger. 'I think she has confirmed to you about our meetings at the allotment. Yes, she told me about her Uncle Jack and his coin collection. But Benny was there as well. She told him.'

'She's been saying that she has barely spoken to Benny.' James remarked quietly.

Jimmy laughed.

'Then why has she been visiting him at his home?'

James and Daye exchanged knowing glances at each other. Was Anne-Marie the mysterious girl friend?

'How do you know that?' James asked tentatively.

'Benny is not very good at writing.' Jimmy began to explain. 'So, he asked Anne-Marie for help. She agreed providing that I wasn't told about it.'

'But Benny did tell you?' James asked quietly.

'He brought a letter into the allotment to show me.' Jimmy began to explain. 'He was applying for a part time job at some call centre in Darwen. It was a well written letter, so I knew that Benny hadn't written it. He'd had some help. And he eventually admitted that Anne-Marie had dictated the letter to him.' Jimmy paused for a few seconds before adding, 'at his home where she frequently visited him.' Jimmy paused again before continuing in a sharp tone of voice. 'And it was during one of those visits that she probably told him all about her uncle Jack and his coin collection.'

'That sounds like a possibility.' James remarked in a non-committal tone of voice.

'You also know about that remark I made about Jessica which was to Anne-Marie.' Jimmy continued in a determined manner. 'But I said it in front of Melanie who wouldn't have repeated it to you because she is afraid of her own shadow.' Jimmy paused again for effect and then added 'Unless, of course, she was being prompted by Anne-Marie.' James' face broke into an involuntary knowing smile. 'I see from your face that that is exactly what happened.'

'There is one big question that I want answering.' James said firmly as he now interrupted Jimmy. 'You say that you have done nothing wrong. In fact, you have said that several times.'

'That's true.' Jimmy shouted.

'Then why have you been in hiding from us the past few days?'

Jimmy smiled. 'I asked for that.'

'Would you care to answer the question?' James pressed.

'After you saw Anne-Marie, she phoned me up.' Jimmy began slowly. 'She'd said that you were looking for me and so advised me to disappear for a while.' Jimmy then looked crestfallen as he looked down at the tabletop. He then angrily added. 'I foolishly did as she advised.'

'And made you look very guilty.' James said not too unkindly at him to which Jimmy nodded solemnly in reply.

At this point James lent back on his chair and began to ponder on what he had heard. Everything that Jimmy had said made sense. The trouble was that none of it was provable in a court of law without the testimony of Benny Gordon and there was no hope of that in the near future. But there was still the question of the disappearance of Jessica Morris. Could Anne-Marie De Wynter be involved in that?

'Were you involved in the disappearance of Jessica Morris?' James suddenly asked as he sat bolt upright facing Jimmy.

'No, I wasn't.' Jimmy said defiantly with more than a trace of anger in his voice.

'We know that you were looking for her on Thursday.' James stated firmly.

'But I never found her.' Jimmy countered fiercely. 'And after talking to Anne-Marie on Friday I stopped looking for her and went into hiding.'

James looked firmly at Jimmy. For once he believed him and began to seriously doubt Anne-Marie De Wynter.

CHAPTER
TWENTY-THREE

★ ★ ★ ★

As James walked briskly into the C.I.D. room he looked towards Daye who was sat at her desk reading the background information on Pamela Frankland.

'I've managed to get Jimmy MacGregor into a bail hostel in Preston.' He said with satisfaction. 'It still makes him look like a suspect which hopefully will keep Anne-Marie De Wynter off guard.'

'We know what Anne-Marie has done,' Daye responded in a less than reassuring voice. 'But we can't prove anything that would stand up in a court of law.'

'Quite correct,' James readily agreed, which brought a look of surprise from Daye. 'So, we'll have to approach this problem from a different direction.'

'Jessica Morris?' Daye offered, but without much conviction in her voice.

'The last time that Jessica was seen alive was Wednesday night.' James began thoughtfully. 'And on the same evening Anne-Marie was seen on her own in the 'Black Bear' at Brymington. Unfortunately, we can't prove that they met up together that night.'

'But we do know that Anne-Marie lied about the reason why she was in the Black Bear that night.' Daye commented adding forcefully, 'It's possible that they did meet up. If only we knew where Anne-Marie went that night.'

'Jimmy and Anne-Marie were regulars in the Black Bear.' James said thoughtfully. 'So maybe there is one person who might just know where she had been to get her shoes so dirty.'

'You don't mean that Welsh waiter, do you?' Daye queried.

'Yes, I do mean Aled.' James responded adding quickly. 'How would you like another meal at the Black bear?'

'Sounds like a good idea.' Daye replied with a smile on her face. 'You might also be interested in Pamela Frankland.' Daye picked up the background information from off her desktop and looked at it. 'As you know Pamela Frankland bought the track suit and balaclava used by the Balaclava Man. We also now know that Tattersall's of Brymington was involved in the financial side of these vehicle thefts.'

'They also have red and white recovery vehicles.' James interrupted. 'Don't forget that.'

'Oh, I haven't. 'Daye replied forcibly. 'And now we have this background information on Pamela Frankland.'

James said nothing in reply but looked quizzically at Daye his eyes imploring her to continue.

'Pamela Frankland is employed by Tattersall's of Brymington.' Daye said in response adding quickly. 'She works in the finance department.'

James' face cracked open into a huge smile.

'I thought you'd be pleased.' Daye remarked. 'So how do you want to play it against Tattersall's?'

'We can't go diving in.' James replied thoughtfully. 'This woman is the only lead we've got. If we spook her, she might just clam up and say nothing and leave us without a plan B.' James then stood looking thoughtful before he added. 'What we need is another source of information at Tattersall's.'

'Have we got time to put someone into Tattersall's undercover?' Daye asked hopefully although her nostrils flared indicating that she was thinking seriously about the prospect.

'Did you say once that we used their recovery vehicles?' James queried.

'Yes, we do.' Daye replied firmly. 'Traffic calls on them if they need a vehicle removing. In fact, I think that Sergeant Absalom could be the officer to talk to. He's frequently in contact with Tattersall's.'

James smiled as he moved towards his desk to start the search for Sergeant Absalom. Several phone calls later and James had completed his task; Sergeant Absalom was in the Police Garage which was next to Templegate.

As James and Daye walked through the Garage doors, they saw amongst the various Police vehicles a red and white recovery vehicle belonging to Tattersall's of Brymington. Several Police officers were surrounding it as a black BMW was being lifted off the back. As it swung in the air the front of the car turned towards James and Daye and they could clearly see that the front left wing had been roughly pushed into the engine block.

'Tried to outrun a patrol car,' a husky voice said to the two C.I.D. officers. 'Then he tried to push an oak tree out of the way. The oak tree didn't move.'

James and Daye turned towards the voice which belonged to a smiling uniformed sergeant.

'I 'm looking for Sergeant Absalom,' James said. 'And as you are the only sergeant in the garage, I assume you must be he.'

Sergeant Absalom gave a slight smile in reply. He clearly did not recognise the C.I.D. officers. James, realising the sergeant's predicament, withdrew his warrant card and showed it to the sergeant.

'Oh, sorry, Sir.' He said apologetically. 'Can I help you?' He then pointed to an office in the corner. 'That's my office over there, Sir.

Sergeant Absalom led the way towards the indicated office which was untidy with papers strewn about the single desk and surrounding wooden chairs. With a sweeping movement of his left hand the burly sergeant brushed the papers off two of the chairs and then indicated to James and Daye to sit down whilst he sat down on a more comfortable chair behind the desk.

'How may I help you, Sir?' The huskily voiced sergeant said to James whilst at the same time opening a desk drawer and withdrawing an orange-coloured lozenge from a paper bag. He showed the lozenge to James. 'Sorry about this, Sir.' He said apologetically. 'But I'll lose my voice completely if I don't have one of these.'

'Caught a nasty bug in the throat?' James asked but not unkindly.

Sergeant Absalom nodded his head in answer before putting the lozenge into his mouth.

'I understand you're the person to talk to about Tattersall's of Brymington?' James asked. 'Do you talk to them a lot?'

'Well, when we need their services, I'm the one that rings them up to book one of their recovery vehicles.' Sergeant Absalom replied with a sucking sound as he sucked on the lozenge. 'May I ask what this is about?'

'It's in connection with the 'balaclava man.' James said quietly but firmly to which Sergeant Absalom raised his bushy eyebrows in surprise. 'We've recently discovered that he's involved with Tattersall's of Brymington. That's why we need to know all we can about their operations and the personnel they employ.'

'What do you want to know?' The sergeant asked huskily but with clear sincerity.

Sergeant Absalom answered James' questions but without his usual smile as he clearly understood the seriousness of the investigation. He told James of the manager of the maintenance division; a workaholic, mid-forties man named Len Fairhead who sometimes drove the recovery vehicles himself although he had about a dozen drivers under him to move the cars, vans and lorries. He was also responsible for the mechanics in the division who repaired and serviced the vehicles.

'What about his personal life?' James asked.

Sergeant Absalom shrugged his shoulders.

'I'm afraid I don't know much about that.' He said apologetically. 'But maybe Tom might know.'

James looked quizzically at the Sergeant.

'He's the driver of the recovery vehicle that's just brought the BMW in.' Sergeant Absalom explained.

James did not immediately reply but thought carefully instead. After all he did not want Fairhead alerted to the fact that the Police were asking questions about him. And Tom might let that slip to his boss.

'Maybe I could ask him.' Daye offered quietly, 'in a roundabout way of course.'

James smiled to Daye as he nodded his head towards her. Daye stood up and walked towards the office door.

As James turned back to face the sergeant, he asked him 'Who else do you deal with at Tattersall's?'

'The only other person I deal with is a woman in the finance department whenever they send us an invoice.' Sergeant Absalom replied almost apologetically because he could not think of anyone else. 'Her name is Pamela Frankland.'

'What can you tell me about her?' James asked in a demanding tone.

Meanwhile Daye was walking up behind a tall burly driver wearing a yellow waterproof vest over his navy-blue jacket. The words on the back of the vest read Tattersall's of Brymington. She tapped the man on the shoulder with her finger.

'Yeah?' he asked gruffly as he turned to face Daye.

Daye looked up into the black weather-beaten face of Tom, a fifties plus worker with bushy greying hair who had obviously spent his working life in the outside air. But he looked fit and healthy although his manner was brusque.

'I bought a car from another garage.' Daye began telling her lie in a very convincing manner. 'And it needs a service. I don't trust the garages mechanics though but a friend of mine said the mechanics at Tattersall's were very good. Can you recommend them?'

Tom looked a little surprised at the question but smiled at Daye as he answered her.

'They've a decent reputation.' He said pleasantly, losing his earlier gruff manner. 'What sort of car have you got?'

'A Mondeo,' Daye lied again.

'Oh, they could do that one alright.' Tom said confidently.

'That's good to know.' Daye smiled back at the Tattersall's driver. 'I was given a name to ask for. A Mrs Fairhead.'

Tom laughed out loud.

'I think you mean Mr Fairhead.' He explained. 'There isn't a Mrs Fairhead anymore. She got kicked into touch years ago. Mind you if you count Pamela from finance, she's been nicknamed Mrs Fairhead for some time now. Len and Pamela have had a thing going for several years.'

'What's she really called?'

'Frankland.' Tom replied.

'I think I've heard that name before.' Daye lied again hoping to get more information out of Tom. 'How long has she worked there?'

'About fifteen years I think.' Tom replied carefully. 'Up until about four years ago when Big Boss Tattersall took her to Lancaster to help sort out some project that he had in the area. Something to do with an art gallery that he was involved with.'

'What made him get involved with an art gallery?' Daye asked curiously, 'a funny project for a garage owner. Did it work out?'

'Of course not,' Tom laughed contemptuously, 'it failed about six months ago and they all came back home.'

'Thanks for that little anecdote.' Daye said as pleasantly as she could. 'But back to my car. How do I book it in?'

Tom laughed as he handed Daye a card.

'Just ring that number and ask for Mr Fairhead.' and then added with a laugh. 'And for God's sake don't call him Mrs.'

Daye laughed as she turned away from Tom. She looked towards Sergeant Absalom's office just as James emerged and so they walked together out of the garage.

'You've done well, Sergeant.' James remarked as they walked slowly back towards Templegate. 'And those dates fit in well with the Balaclava Man's activities.'

'Could it just be the two of them?' Daye queried, her nostrils flaring as she thought deeply about it. 'Or have Fairhead and Frankland had an accomplice?'

'Good question.' James replied thoughtfully. 'Let's see what Qasim can come up with first.'

CHAPTER
TWENTY-FOUR

The road to the Black Bear went past the site of Tattersall's of Brymington with the car showrooms on the left and the maintenance division on the right. Daye looked wistfully at both parts of the site, her nostrils flaring as she thought deeply about the Balaclava Man. She knew that they were close to catching him but only if they caught him red handed. Daye silently prayed to Qasim.

Daye wondered about the Black Bear. She turned towards James who was driving his Mondeo towards Brymington. She understood the reason for seeing Aled at the Black Bear but why the meal? A quick look at her wristwatch told her that the time was 11;47. *Close to lunchtime she had to admit but was there more to it? Secretly she was hoping that there was.*

Once at the Black Bear James parked his Mondeo on the car park before walking silently to the front door of the restaurant. Daye walked just as silently beside him as they entered the old but brightly coloured building.

The lunchtime crowd had not descended on the Black Bear as shown by the near total desertion of the eating area.

'Mr. Buchan.' a jovial voice greeted James in its distinctive Welsh Accent.

'Hello, Aled.' James replied cordially. 'I hope you are ready for lunchtime trade.' He remarked in a flippant manner as he looked around the empty tables in the restaurant.

'The lunchtime crowd from Tattersall's usually don't get in for another half hour yet.' Aled replied with a faint trace of a smile. 'Would you like the same table as last time?'

James smiled broadly as he nodded a reply in the affirmative and followed Aled over to their table.

James and Daye took their seats at the table and declined the offered menus. James requested his favourite steak and ale pie while Daye went for a cheese omelette and side salad. As Aled opened his mouth to enquire as to what drinks they would like James laughingly interrupted him with a firm 'two specials please, Aled.'

Daye watched the smiling Aled disappear into the kitchen. As the kitchen door closed, Daye turned to look into the face of James who was looking intently at her.

'I must say I quite like the Black Bear.' Daye said quietly, 'I'd like to come here again.'

'Maybe we will.' James replied softly, his blue green eyes looking deep into Daye's brown ones, 'When we're not on duty.'

Daye smiled at James but did not say anything. She did not need too.

Aled returned to the table carrying a tray with two long glasses of amber liquid on it. He placed the glasses on the table beside James and Daye.

'Two specials as ordered, Mr Buchan.' Aled said. 'Your meals won't be too long in coming.'

As Aled turned towards the kitchen James took hold of his arm.

'Just a quick word please, Aled.' James said quietly but firmly.

Aled said nothing but looked quizzically at James.

'Pull up a chair.' James commanded.

Aled did as he was told and pulled up a chair placing it next to James before sitting on it and looking steely eyed at the Police Inspector.

'Last time we spoke,' James began quietly. 'You told me about Anne-Marie De Wynter.'

Aled nodded his agreement before adding firmly, 'That was about her last visit to the Black Bear.'

'Correct.' James quickly agreed. 'But I want to ask you about her shoes. Where had she been walking before she came here that night?'

Aled screwed up his eyes as though in surprise but did not speak immediately.

'Her shoes were muddy.' He said slowly and thoughtfully. 'Not surprising as there are some good country walks around here.'

'What about the scuff marks?' James probed. 'You don't get them from mud.'

'That's true.' Aled readily agreed. 'But you do get them from Gravel. And I do know that Miss De Wynter liked to take a walk around the gravel pits along Badgers Halt Road.'

'Is there a gravel pit big enough to hide a car in?'

Aled thought carefully before he answered.

'There are a couple that could hide a car.' He began saying slowly and deliberately. 'But the best place would be at Hunter's Quarry. There's a lake there now. That's what stopped the quarrying. I don't know the depth of the lake but I'm sure the water could hide a car. I'd start my search there.'

'Thank you, Aled.' James said with a broad smile on his face. He knew where Hunter's Quarry was. 'We'll have our lunch first and then start searching there.'

'An excellent idea, Mr. Buchan' Aled said as he stood up. 'I'll just go and check on your meals for you.' Aled turned away and noticed the door of the restaurant open and several people enter. 'Looks like the Tattersall's people are early.'

Aled went towards the kitchen door while James and Daye looked at the newcomers.

Suddenly Daye froze as a small group of people walked past her table; for in the middle of the group was Tom, the Tattersall's recovery driver.

'Oh, hiya.' Tom said as he noticed Daye. 'Did you get your car booked in alright?'

'Not had time yet.' Daye replied sheepishly.

Tom stood beside Daye while the rest of the group went towards a table in the corner.

'See that man at the table next to the bar?' he said to Daye, pointing towards a couple taking their seats at the table. 'That's Len Fairhead.'

Daye looked at the man. He was mid-forties, balding with greyish hair, stocky build with a paunch which showed that he liked to eat well and did not exercise. As to his height Daye could only guess as he was sat down but he did not look tall.

'Who's the woman with him?' she asked quietly.

'That's Mrs. Fairhead.' Tom replied with a hearty laugh. 'Enjoy your meal.' He added as he turned towards his friends in the corner.

Daye had a good look at Pamela Frankland who was sat opposite Len Fairhead. She looked thirty plus with a trim figure. Her black hair, which looked dyed, was short cropped and tidy. She did not look particularly tall but again Daye would have to guess her height.

Fortunately for Daye neither of them had noticed the intense scrutiny that Daye was giving them. So, this was the pair that was possibly behind the Balaclava Man, thought Daye, or was she wrong?

From her seat Daye had an uninterrupted view of Fairhead and Frankland. James had his back to them so could not look at them without making it look obvious that he was spying on them, but Daye could study them at leisure using James' body as a shield.

When their meals arrived James and Daye chose to eat in silence so that they could overhear the conversations that the Tattersall's people were having. Unfortunately, they could not hear clearly what Fairhead and Frankland were saying as they had chosen to speak in soft tones.

When they had finished their meals James and Daye rose silently to leave. They walked quietly towards the exit, stopping only at the cashier's desk to pay their bill. After a quick goodbye to Aled, who was attending to customers at a nearby table, James and Daye left the restaurant.

Once outside the Black Bear James and Daye hurried towards the car park where they sat in the Mondeo.

'What do you think?' James asked as he looked demandingly at Daye.

Daye's nostrils flared as she thought carefully about what to reply.

'I don't think either Fairhead or Frankland actually knew that we are onto them.' She said slowly. 'After all, neither of them paid us any attention in there.'

'Neither did anyone else.' James remarked. 'All their conversations seemed to be about work.'

'Then we are still in the hands of Qasim?' Daye asked.

'Yes.' James replied firmly. 'I'll contact him when we get back to Templegate. But first let's get to Hunters Quarry.'

James pressed the accelerator of the Mondeo and turned off the car park and towards Badgers Halt Road.

As the entrance to the quarry appeared on the right-hand side of the road James turned off the tarmac road and onto a muddy gravel track. He drove past a battered and broken wooden gate which held up a dirty and graffiti covered sign welcoming people to Hunter's Quarry. Vandals must have visited the site since it closed as the gate was now held open by a pair of broken breeze blocks.

James drove carefully along the potholed and rocky track as he made his way up a slight incline. Ahead of them, slowly coming into view was the lake.

'God that looks eerie!' Daye said gloomily as she looked at the black surface of the lake which looked miserable and foreboding.

'Yes.' James agreed. 'But we can get a better view from up there.'

Daye looked at where James was pointing his finger. It was a cliff edge overlooking the lake. James drove carefully up the incline to the top of the cliff and turned his car towards the lake but stopped about fifteen feet from the edge.

James and Daye exited the Mondeo and began searching the mud splattered grass that covered the top of the cliff.

Other vehicles had parked there previously as shown by tyre tracks in the mud. They too had parked about fifteen feet from the edge except for one set of tyre tracks that Daye had noticed.

'These tracks go right up to the edge.' She said firmly as she studied the muddy imprint of the tyres. 'And they don't look like they reversed away again afterwards.'

James moved over towards Daye and examined the tyre tracks and readily agreed with her deduction.

'They're definitely the tracks of a saloon car.'

'Perhaps from a Toyota do you think?'

'I can't tell that.' James said quietly. 'But it could be a car of that size.'

James then walked over to the edge of the cliff and looked down into the inky blackness of the lake. He then carefully studied the tyre tracks as they went over the edge.

'Seen something?' Daye asked as she came over and stood beside James.

'The reason why there are no signs of the car reversing is because it went straight over the edge.' James said solemnly. 'Look at the edge. As the car went over it took some mud and grass with it.'

Daye looked down at where James had just been studying and saw where the grass had been pulled out of the ground. She then looked down at the lake.

'It's about fifty feet down into that black soup which could easily hide any vehicle.' James said to her. 'When we get back to Templegate I'll contact Superintendent Edwards about getting us the underwater search team.' He then added ominously. 'And rather them then me to go into that black soup.'

CHAPTER
TWENTY-FIVE

★ ★ ★ ★

James drove his Mondeo onto the car park at Templegate and parked near the entrance of the police station. As Daye exited the vehicle, she pointed with her index finger at a smartly dressed uniformed officer walking towards a shiny new jaguar car. James looked at who Daye was pointing at.

'Superintendent Edwards.' He said firmly. 'Just the man I'm after.'

Without hesitation James ran towards the senior officer.

Superintendent Edwards, a well-built man in his fifties with greying hair and a slight paunch, turned towards James and stopped.

'There's no need to rush Inspector.' The senior officer said as James drew close. 'I'm on my way to a budget review meeting where I hope to get the money for a couple of new officers for you. I've even got a couple of candidates lined up.'

'That's good news, Sir.' James said excitedly and showing his approval with a huge grin on his face. He then added firmly. 'I also need an underwater search unit.'

'What!' Edwards bellowed. 'What do you want that for?'

'You know we are looking for a missing woman called Jessica Morris?'

'I've read the reports.' Edwards snapped. 'What of it?'

'We've just come from Hunter's Quarry, Sir.' James replied quickly. 'There is evidence that a car has recently gone into the lake there. And based on other evidence we believe that Jessica could be in that car.'

Superintendent Edwards looked thoughtful as he stood silent for a few moments.

'OK.' He suddenly said. 'I'll get your frogmen for you. Now can I go to my meeting?'

'Of course, Sir' James respectfully replied. 'And thank you.'

Superintendent Edwards hurried towards his Jaguar car where his immaculately dressed chauffer had already opened a rear passenger door for him. Edwards quickly climbed into the back of the vehicle.

Daye walked up to James and stood beside him and watched the speedily departing Jaguar as it raced off the car park.

'Did I hear right, Sir?' Daye asked slowly as though unsure how to ask. 'Could we be getting some extra officers?'

'If all goes well' James replied with a smile, but added cautiously, 'Keep that under your hat for the time being.'

James and Daye smiled at each other as they entered the police station.

'Interview room.' the desk sergeant said to James and Daye as they walked past him. 'Your friend Qasim has something for you.'

The two officers hurried towards the interview room where they found Qasim Patel sat at the table drinking a cup of tea: his briefcase lying half open on the table. He politely stood up as James and Daye entered the room.

'Good afternoon, Qasim.' James said with a huge grin on his face. 'I hope we haven't kept you waiting long.'

'Not at all, Sir' Qasim replied. He was polite but unsmiling. 'I'm certain you'd want to hear my news. King Kong has been busy last night.'

James' face immediately took on a serious expression. He told everyone to sit down with Qasim sitting opposite James and Daye.

'What's King Kong been doing?' James urgently demanded to know.

'He started at about eleven o'clock last night going through the latest request forms.' Qasim began slowly and clearly. He produced at copy of one request form from out of his briefcase. 'This is one of the request forms that caught his eye. It's from a garage in Oxford.'

James took hold of the copy.

'A Renault Clio,' he said firmly as he studied the details of the wanted vehicle. 'Has he gone looking for one?'

'Yes.' Qasim replied, pulling another copy out of his briefcase. 'He's been looking into some archives of garages connected with A.V.I.S. He found that in a garage in Preston. The firm is called Glendale Used Cars.'

Qasim handed the archive copy over to James.

'This car was sold by Glendale just four months ago to a Mrs Hanley of Rochester Avenue.' James read from the copy. He continued. 'It's less than two years old. Mrs. Hanley is a divorcee with one child and wants the car for work, shopping and doing the school run.' James turned to Daye. 'Sounds like a perfect victim for the balaclava man. Better do an urgent background check on her.'

Daye immediately stood up. 'I'll do it straight away, Sir.' And with that she quickly hurried to the door and left.

'You've done well Qasim.' James said in a complimentary manner.

'Thank you, Sir.' Qasim replied politely, but once again without a smile. 'Is there anything more I can do for you?'

'Just keep monitoring King Kong for the time being.' James said thoughtfully, and then added carefully, 'just in case he changes his mind in any way.'

Qasim nodded his head but said nothing.

'And now you can tell me what is wrong with you?'

Qasim looked at James in surprise.

'Don't look at me like that.' James admonished. 'You've got a problem. what is it?'

Qasim smiled slightly before replying. 'I'm not sure that I'll be able to hold Whittingham Computer Systems together after we catch the Balaclava Man.'

'What makes you say that?' James Queried.

'I am the only member of the triumvirate that's left.' Qasim said sadly. 'Nigel is a long way from recovering from his broken leg, and poor old John Tomlinson has given up hope of saving the reputation of the A.V.I.S. program when the full story of how the Balaclava Man used the system to steal vehicles and target those women to assault gets out. He's convinced that the garages and the customers will lose faith in us.'

'Not necessarily.' James replied reassuringly. 'Look how you've helped us. I'll certainly make sure that you get the credit that you deserve.'

'Thanks for that, Mr. Buchan.' Qasim said with another slight smile. 'But we'll just have to wait and see what the future holds'

Qasim closed his briefcase and slowly headed for the door. His last look back at Inspector Buchan was a sad smile. James could only smile back.

After leaving the interview room James went back to the C.I.D. room where he saw a smiling Daye putting down the phone's receiver.

'You're looking happy.' James said in a jovial manner. 'Got anything good?'

'I should say so' She replied excitedly. 'As you know Mrs. Hanley is a divorcee. I've just been talking to her ex-husband who happens to be a Detective Inspector in Preston. He's very keen to help us but he wants to talk to you first.'

'What's his number?' James demanded to know as he hurried towards his own desk.

'You don't need to know it.' Daye said just as James picked up his own phone. 'D.I. Hanley is coming over here. He should be here in less than an hour.'

'He's keen to help, isn't he?' James said warily as he put his phone back down. 'How's he connected with these cases?'

'That I do not know.' Daye replied cautiously. 'But I think we'll get the answer to that quite soon.'

The phone rang on James' desk. James picked up the receiver.

'Buchan.' He said bluntly into the mouthpiece and then listened to the voice at the other end. 'That's good news sergeant. Do you know where Hunter's Quarry is?' James smiled as he listened to the answer. 'Excellent.' James said proudly. 'We'll meet you there at nine.'

James was smiling as he put the phone down.

Turning towards Daye he said, 'That was the underwater search unit. They had a training day scheduled for tomorrow but as they've dived at Hunter's Quarry before they know what to expect. So, we are meeting them there tomorrow morning at nine o'clock.'

'Excellent.' Daye exclaimed. 'But before that I think we ought to prepare for D.I. Hanley's visit.'

James readily agreed and spent the next fifty-three minutes going through the paperwork with Daye.

It was with a flourish that the desk sergeant entered the C.I.D. room followed by a smartly dressed man wearing a grey suit. He was well built with a full head of dark hair. James estimated his age as early thirties.

'This is Detective Inspector Hanley from Preston, Sir.' The desk sergeant said to James who advanced towards Hanley with an outstretched hand.

'I'm D.I Buchan.' James said in a welcoming manner. 'Just call me James. And' He added turning to Daye. 'This is D.S. Durham.'

'Good afternoon, Sergeant.' Hanley said as he shook her hand. 'I believe you're called Daisy. I'm called Doug.'

Daye grimaced but said nothing.

'She doesn't like to be called Daisy.' James quickly explained. 'She prefers Daye'

'Then Daye it is.' Doug smiled.

'Please sit-down, Doug' James offered pointing to a nearby chair. 'And would you like a drink?'

'Oh no, thanks.' Doug replied sitting down on the offered chair. 'I'd rather just get on with discussing the Balaclava Man.'

'Good man.' James exclaimed whilst signalling to the desk sergeant that he could leave which he immediately did. 'But first of all, what do you know of him?'

'I know what he did to my sister-in-law.' Doug said solemnly with more than a hint of anger. 'She was my ex-wife's sister, Valerie Clark.'

'Oh, good grief.' Daye responded. 'Then you know what sort of man we are dealing with.'

'Yes, I do.' Doug replied and then added vehemently. 'And both myself and Elaine, my ex-wife, saw how she suffered and that's why we'll both do whatever we can to catch this monster.'

'I fully understand and appreciate what you've said Doug.' James said cautiously. 'But are you aware of exactly how he operates?'

Doug looked quizzically at James as he asked, 'How do you mean?'

'You have a child with Elaine I believe?'

'That's right.' Doug replied warily. He was obviously unsure as to where this question was leading. 'We have an eight-year-old daughter, Natalie. But what has she got to do with anything?'

James and Daye exchanged mournful glances. It was Daye that spoke next.

'The Balaclava Man uses the children of his victims like a lever to force the women to do what he wants.' Daye spoke softly and sincerely; then she added soulfully. 'He puts a knife to their throats. Once a mother sees that she will do anything to prevent her child from being hurt.'

'Oh my God.' Doug exclaimed. 'I didn't know that. As for Elaine and me we'll do whatever is necessary to catch this man, but I can't .... won't .... Risk my daughter's life.'

'No one would expect you to, Doug.' James said firmly. 'I've got two daughters' myself, so I know exactly what you mean.'

'Then how are you going to trap him?' Doug asked quizzically.

'We've got to make him believe that a child is in the car when in actual fact there isn't one there.' James said carefully although he obviously wasn't sure how.

'Could I just make a suggestion at this point, Sir?' Daye interjected from her seat behind her desk. 'I haven't mentioned this before because I'm still working on it in my mind.'

'You've got an idea, Daye?'

'Yes, I have, Sir.' She replied flaring her nostrils as she spoke. 'I know a woman of twenty-five who is physically fit and knows self-defence.'

'I know lots of policewomen that match that description.' It was Doug that had interrupted Daye. 'But they wouldn't pass for an eight-year-old.'

'Emily would.' Daye replied with a knowing smile. 'She is only four feet tall'

'A midget' James exclaimed as he sat bolt upright and looked aghast as he faced Daye.

'She prefers to be called a small person.' Daye corrected him politely. 'Actually, she suffers from a form of dwarfism.

But dress her up in the correct clothes and she would pass for an eight-year-old.'

'At four feet tall she can't be a policewoman.' James objected forcefully. 'We can't ask a civilian to do a job like this.'

'And why can't we use her for goodness' sake?' Daye asked innocently. 'We obviously can't use a real child and policewomen are too tall.'

James sat silently looking at Daye as he thought over her suggestion.

'She's got a point you know.' Doug said hopefully but added as a warning. 'But what your superintendent Edwards would say I wouldn't like to guess at.'

James turned towards Doug before turning silently back to face Daye.

'Have you approached this woman?'

'Not yet.' Daye replied calmly. 'But we do have something to offer her.'

James looked quizzically at her.

'Emily's parents own a corner shop in Bellingham.' Daye continued slowly and calmly. 'They've been raided by a masked man wielding a baseball bat. The case is not being investigated properly. If I could promise to prioritise the investigation, I'm fairly certain that she would help us.'

James stood up and walked slowly and thoughtfully towards the window behind his desk. He then turned to face Daye.

'You're putting forward a very good argument.' He said wistfully to her. 'But what would Edwards say to it? Because if this goes wrong and, Heaven forbids, someone gets hurt or worse, all three of us could be facing charges.'

'And what would happen if we did nothing?' Doug queried. 'I don't want to see another woman end up like my sister-in-law. She didn't deserve what happened to her.'

James slowly nodded his head. Doug has just put forward the most compelling argument of all. But it would all now depend on the planning; and it would have to be careful and meticulous planning with nothing left to chance. It was now up to Doug to begin that planning with information about his ex-wife's movements; Movements that included his daughter Natalie.

CHAPTER
TWENTY-SIX

★ ★ ★ ★

The light rain fell as a drizzle as Daye crossed the car park heading for the Mondeo where James sat waiting for her. Behind her was the swimming pool where Daye had left a smiling Emily enjoying her morning dip in the cool water; The idea of helping the police to capture the Balaclava Man had appealed to Emily's adventurous spirit; but she had also been pleased with the offer of prioritising the investigation into the robbery of her parents' corner shop. At this point it was Daye's turn to smile as Daye felt certain that Emily would have volunteered to be a decoy anyway. But Daye was pleased that Emily would be rewarded.

As Daye approached the Mondeo, she could see through the windscreen that James was talking on his mobile phone. He ended the conversation as Daye opened the passenger door and entered the vehicle.

'She's in.' Daye exclaimed excitedly. 'I felt sure she'd go for it.'

'I've just been talking to Doug.' James remarked but not as excitedly as Daye had been. 'Both he and Elaine are up for it, but the problem is Natalie. They don't want her to be put at risk in any shape or form.' He then added soulfully, 'which is perfectly understandable, of course.'

'Well, she won't be will she?' Daye said firmly. 'We've got Emily.'

'Yes of course.' James said optimistically. 'He wants to meet us in Templegate later this morning. I think he's got one or two ideas to put to us.'

Daye looked at her watch. 'It's 8-51, Sir. Time we were heading for Hunter's Quarry.'

James nodded his head in acknowledgement and started the mondeo's engine. He drove carefully off the car park before speeding up and hurrying towards Brymington. At 8-59 precisely James entered the track that led to the quarry.

On the cliff top overlooking the lake was a single police car with two officers stood beside it. Two police vans were at the bottom of the hill beside the lake with several officers preparing for a dive. A rubber dingy, complete with outboard motor, several oxygen tanks, and various ropes lay on the ground beside the van whilst close by was parked a large mobile crane.

'It looks like they've come prepared.' James remarked on the sight as he drove his car up the hill towards the single police vehicle. He parked his Mondeo next to the two officers who looked suspiciously at him.

James and Daye got out and approached the two men.

'D.I. Buchan and,' James pointed to Daye, 'D.S. Durham.' He spoke to the burley officer with the sergeant's stripes.

'Morning, Sir.' The sergeant respectfully greeted his superior officer. 'Campbell is the name and,' turning towards his fellow officer, 'this is Constable Rees. He's dived here before and reckons this is a good spot to dump a car.'

'Have you had a look around, Rees?' James asked the lean and young-looking constable.

'Yes, Sir.' The Constable replied in a soft Lancashire accent. He then pointed to the tyre tracks on the ground. 'Despite the rain recently the tracks are still clear, and they lead right over the edge.'

The small group of officers walked to the edge of the cliff top where Constable Rees pointed downwards to a spot directly below them.

'There's a crater directly below us at a depth of about thirty feet.' He said quietly. 'The chances are that any vehicle going over this edge would be at the bottom of that crater. What vehicle would we be looking for?'

'It's a white Toyota.' It was Daye who replied. 'And we think there might be a woman inside it.'

'Right,' the constable said firmly. 'If she's down there we'll find her.'

With that the sergeant and constable went back to their vehicle and drove towards the other police vehicles at the lakeside.

'You stay here Daye and report on anything they find.' James ordered. 'I'll go back to Templegate and contact Doug Hanley.'

James drove Daye down the hill to join up with the underwater search unit. He then left to return to Templegate.

As James drove onto the Templegate car park he was surprised, and pleased, to see Doug Hanley exiting a car near the entrance.

James ran after Doug and caught up with him just as he went through the door into the foyer of the police station.

'You've timed that perfectly Doug.' He said to him as Doug was about to talk to the desk sergeant. Doug turned around to face a smiling James. 'Let's go up to the C.I.D. room.'

Once inside the C.I.D. room James headed for the coffee machine.

'Do you fancy a coffee?' James asked casually although he was eager to know what Doug had to say.

'Please.' Doug replied, 'with one sugar.'

James prayed for the water to boil faster than normal but of course it would not. When the coffee was ready, he handed a cup to Doug who was sat down opposite James' desk. James then took the other cup and sat down behind his desk.

'I had a good long talk with Elaine last night.' Doug said firmly. 'And I think I have found a solution to our problem with Natalie.'

'That's good.' James enthused. 'What is the solution?'

'We went through all the scenarios possible.' Doug spoke in a methodical voice. 'Elaine must do the school run every day. Natalie goes to St. Francis primary on Astbury Road which is usually gridlocked morning and afternoon. That is caused by St. Mark's secondary school being on the same road.'

'That would be too risky for the Balaclava Man.' James said quietly. 'He likes a quick getaway. A traffic jam would not be helpful to him at all.'

'That's what I thought.' Doug quickly agreed and then added sharply 'Elaine also takes Natalie with her to do the weekly shopping on a Saturday morning at Walton's Hypermarket.'

'I know that place.' James interrupted quickly. 'The entire complex is surrounded by a wire fence and CCTV cameras and the car park gates are closed electronically by the security guards operating the cameras. He'd never get away with a kidnapping in that car park.'

'But I think I know where he would make an attempt.'

James quickly fell silent and looked quizzically at Doug.

'But it does depend on if you've got Emily to replace Natalie.'

'We have.' James said firmly. 'Daye spoke to her this morning. And Daye tells me that she can look after herself.'

'Good.' Doug said quietly, obviously relieved that a deputy had been found for Natalie. 'Do you know Cranberry Hall on Duke's Road in Bellingham?'

'Of course, I do.' James replied firmly, obviously irritated at the suggestion that he did not know his own town. 'It's used as a community centre. There's a dance club there that both my daughters used to attend.'

'My Natalie does attend it.' Doug responded just as firmly. 'She receives private tuition from Mrs. Honeycutt after the normal club has finished. Natalie must be there for eleven o'clock. Elaine takes her there straight after doing the shopping.'

'She'll be on her own at that time.' James remarked. 'The club itself used to finish at ten thirty.'

'It still does.'

'How long is her private tuition?'

'One hour.'

'Who's on the car park at twelve o'clock?'

Doug smiled before answering, 'just a couple of cars that belong to the hall staff. They're usually there all day especially if there is an event on that evening.' Doug then looked at a map on the wall next to James' desk. He stood up and approached the map.

'This is Duke's Road.' He said pointing to a straight road of about two miles in length. 'Cranberry Hall is about halfway down on the North side.'

'That's right.' James agreed, standing up to be beside Doug. 'There's a line of parking bays at the side of the road next to a path that leads through some trees up to the entrance.'

'Elaine normally parks in one of those bays.' Doug said quietly. 'But I don't know much about the rest of the land that surrounds the hall.'

'There are two other car parks.' James began to explain. 'The main car park is too the right of the hall and is only opened for big occasions. The other car park to the left is for deliveries only.'

'That makes sense.' Doug interrupted. 'The kitchens, cafe and the storerooms are on that side of the hall.' He suddenly added quickly. 'What's round the back?'

'Two tennis courts and a bowling green,' James answered firmly. 'And cut off from the trees beyond by a wire fence that has only one gate that is big enough for one person to get through at a time.'

Doug smiled as he stroked his chin and looked thoughtful.

'I think I know how he is going to do it.' He suddenly said causing James to look quizzically at him. 'He's going to enter Cranberry Hall through the back and just walk right through to the front.'

'And then down the path to the parking bays.' James added forcefully.

'What could look more innocent?' Doug asked. 'It would look perfectly natural.'

'He could approach Elaine's car without looking the slightest bit suspicious.' James agreed. 'But where could we hide to protect Elaine?'

'If Elaine parked in one of the end bays to the left of the path,' Doug pointed to the bays on the map and then moved his finger to the delivery car park. 'We could hide in an unmarked Police van here. We would be less than a hundred yards from Elaine.'

'Perfect.' James enthused. 'There would be no escape. To the South is nothing but a brick wall with an industrial estate behind it; and we could block both ends of Dukes Road with Police cars. He's trapped.' But James quickly added, 'but what about Natalie?'

'I'll arrange with Elaine for a swap with Emily somewhere on the road from the hypermarket.' Doug responded and added firmly. 'And it all takes place this Saturday.'

Over at Hunter's Quarry Daye was watching a white Toyota being winched out of the murky waters of the lake. Water was gushing out of its broken windows and wheel arches. Daye's heart was beating fast and felt heavy and sad as she watched it being lowered onto the ground beside a recovery vehicle. The diver had reported that there was a woman's body inside

CHAPTER
TWENTY-SEVEN

Daye Durham stood silently beside the double doors of the pathology lab in the hospital mortuary whilst she watched the pathologist, and her assistants examine the body lying on the centre table. She had seen these examinations before, but her stomach still felt queasy and wanting to do cartwheels. Daye watched Dr. Sinclair, the plump female pathologist with a wrinkled face and grey hair showing below her blue hospital cap as she opened the chest cavity of the female corpse. Her blue gown and white apron were already streaked with blood stains which looked like mini red rivers flowing down the front of her hospital attire. One assistant was standing beside her making notes on a clipboard whilst another assistant was examining the contents of a brown handbag that had been found in the Toyota.

The double doors silently opened and a hand, just as silently, reached in and touched Daye on her left shoulder. As she turned to see the owner of the hand a finger was raised and beckoned her to come outside.

'Good morning, Sir.' She said politely to her superior officer. 'I'm not exactly keen on watching the next bit.'

James looked into the lab and grimaced as he saw Dr. Sinclair fold back the opening of the chest cavity and peer at the woman's internal organs.

'Oh God. I see what you mean.' James said with a look of disgust on his face. 'Let's go outside for some fresh air.'

Once outside the mortuary the two officers breathed in the smell of clean air and the fragrance of freshly cut grass which was damp from the morning dew.

'Have they discovered anything yet?' James quietly asked Daye who had once again tied her hair back into a ponytail.

'They've confirmed her identity as Jessica Morris.' Daye replied sadly, obviously still upset at what was happening to her body in the pathology lab. 'Though actually I already knew it was her. I recognised her yesterday when they took her out of the Toyota.' Daye took a deep breath before continuing. 'How was your meeting with Superintendent Edwards?'

'It went well.' James said, the tone of surprise in his voice was unmistakeable. 'He has agreed to Doug's plan, and we go tomorrow.'

'Isn't that a bit soon?' Daye queried. 'I know that there are going to be road works nearby but......'

'The road works are a problem.' James interrupted. 'Those collapsed pipes under London Road are more extensive than was first thought. They start work on the repairs next Monday and it could be several weeks before the repairs are completed. In the meantime, traffic will be diverted along Dukes Road.'

'That could cause a few traffic jams.' Daye observed.

'Precisely,' agreed James. 'And the Balaclava Man won't like that.'

'So, it has to be tomorrow or not at all.' Daye said solemnly. 'What's the plan for tomorrow?'

'Natalie will go with her mother to Walton's hypermarket while Doug will collect Emily from her home. Emily will be given clothes identical to what Natalie will be wearing.' James's voice was serious and careful, but his facial expression showed signs of worry. He was obviously considering what could go wrong as he had not mentioned to Superintendent Edwards the part that Natalie and Emily would be playing. 'This plan would be either successful or else you and I will be looking to begin new careers.' James said anxiously before continuing. 'Elaine and Doug will meet up in a lay-by just outside of Bellingham. Natalie and Emily, now dressed in identical clothes, will change vehicles. Natalie, now with her father, will be taken to Doug's home for safe keeping while Elaine and Emily drive to Cranberry Hall where Elaine will park in a bay to the left of the footpath. They will then enter Cranberry Hall where you and another officer will pretend to be parents waiting for your child to appear. What you really will be doing will be keeping a close eye on Elaine and Emily.'

'From inside the hall?' queried Daye.

'Doug believes that the Balaclava Man will enter the hall at the rear and exit by the front door to get to the parking bays.'

'Surely he wouldn't try anything in the hall, would he?'

'I doubt it. Remember, it's the car he's after.' James said reassuringly to her. 'I'm just not taking any chances. Once he closes in on Elaine's car that's when we pounce. He won't be able to escape as we'll have two unmarked police cars blocking both ends of Duke's Road and I'll be in radio contact with everybody from my position in the unmarked police van parked in the delivery bays.'

'What about the recovery vehicle from Tattersall's?' Daye asked quietly. 'Will we be able to find it?'

'We should be able to trace it using CCTV once the vehicle turns towards the Duke's Road area.'

'It sounds good, Sir.' Daye said confidently obviously aware that James was having some doubts and so she was trying to boost his confidence about the plan. 'I think we've got everything covered,' she said with a smile.

The door to the morgue opened quietly behind them.

'Dr. Sinclair has some information for you, Inspector.'

James and Daye turned towards the sound of the voice which belonged to one of Dr. Sinclair's assistants. Without saying another word, the assistant turned and led the two police officers back towards the pathology lab. Once inside the lab the two were confronted by Dr. Sinclair who was removing her face mask but still wore her blood-stained apron.

'Right, Inspector,' she said gruffly. 'I suppose your D.S Cleveland here has confirmed to you that the deceased is indeed called Jessica Morris.'

'Durham,' interrupted Daye who was not disguising her irritation at her mispronounced surname. 'I'm called D.S. Durham.'

'Oh, sorry I thought it was Cleveland.' The pathologist replied in a matter of fact and patronising voice. 'I knew it was some place in the Northeast.'

'We have been informed of the deceased surname thank you Doctor.' James said quickly whilst looking sideways at Daye as much as to say, '*Shut up and don't get involved in a silly argument.*'

Daye took the hint and said nothing although her nostrils flared because she was thinking of some choice words to use towards Dr. Sinclair the next time they should meet.

'Can you tell us how she died?' James asked Dr. Sinclair.

'It was definitely by drowning.' She replied sharply. 'But she didn't put up a struggle. Hand me those flasks will you Alison?'

Dr. Sinclair turned to one of her assistants as she spoke. The young assistant picked up two medium sized thermos flasks and handed them to Dr. Sinclair who held them up for James to see.

'Both flasks contain coffee.' She said firmly. 'But you will notice that one flask has a piece of tape attached to it but the other one does not.'

James looked closely at the flasks. So did Daye.

'One of those flasks contains more than just coffee.' James said with conviction.

'Correct.' Dr. Sinclair agreed, 'but which one? I poured some of the coffee from each flask into two cups. The coffee from the flask with the tape was a slightly darker colour than the contents from the other flask. Therefore, I suspect that the flask with the tape contains some sort of sedative. I've sent a sample of the contents to be analysed but I'm sure I'm right. I'll let you know the results when I get them.'

'Where did you get the flasks from?' James asked looking at Alison the assistant.

Alison picked up a brown handbag and handed it to James along with a pair of white surgical gloves.

'This was found in the Toyota.' She said soberly and without emotion. 'There are other items in it which you may want to look at.'

James put the gloves on before taking hold of the handbag and placing it on a nearby table so he could examine its contents. Daye stood beside him and helped him to examine a shopping list, a newspaper, a bulletin about a church bazaar, and something gleaming from inside a pocket on the inside of the handbag. James removed the object from the pocket and held it in the palm of his hand as he looked at the white enamel brooch with a shiny silver cross emblazoned in its centre. He turned the brooch over and read the inscription on the reverse side:

> *To My God Daughter Ann*
> *May the Saints Watch over you*
> *From your loving God Father Jack*

'Now who do we know called Ann and Jack?' James said to Daye with a straight face. It was a question that did not require an answer.

The reception room of Danby and Sons (engineering) Ltd. was clean and tidy. Anne-Marie De Wynter had watched several applicants enter and leave the door marked Human Resources, but she was sat patiently awaiting her turn to be interviewed. She had applied for the job of receptionist the day after an angry Mr. Ashcroft had stormed into her office and had fired her on the spot citing 'inappropriate behaviour' and finishing with 'and don't ask for a reference.'

Only a few applicants were still left waiting outside the human resources office when a young well-dressed man entered the reception room and spoke to the mature receptionist on duty. He handed her a newspaper and pointed to an article on an inside page.

'Good grief.' She said softly. 'When did this happen?'

'Yesterday,' the young man replied excitedly. 'My brother works at Tattersall's and saw the car coming out of the water.'

'You're not talking about that car the police found in Hunter's Quarry, are you?' a timid voice from among the applicants said, 'It said later on the radio that there was a body found inside it.'

Anne-Marie suddenly sat bolt upright on her chair.

'That surely can't be Jessica.' She thought anxiously to herself. *'Nobody could possibly have known about her being in the lake, and certainly not the police.'*

'It doesn't mention anything about a body in here.' The mature receptionist said referring to the article in the paper. 'It just says the car was a white Toyota.'

Anne-Marie felt a sickness well up in her stomach.

It can't be. She thought desperately to herself, *a white Toyota and a body.* Anne-Marie could feel the colour drain from her cheeks. *The police are still holding Benny and Jimmy. They know it was Jimmy who killed Jessica, but Jimmy doesn't know about her body being in the lake at Hunter's Quarry. Oh God I'm getting confused. What's going on here? It must be a coincidence.*

Anne-Marie listened quietly to the ongoing conversation about the car in the lake. Some of the applicants were putting forward theories; some of them quite outlandish; about what had happened and who was the person found in the vehicle. This was a rather pointless theory as no one even knew the sex of the victim. But all the talk in the room was upsetting for Ann-Marie which was adding to her confusion. She did not contribute to the conversation but remained silent throughout. No one even noticed her as she quietly got up and left the room. Her mind was in a shroud of fog as she walked aimlessly along the streets of Bellingham.

CHAPTER
TWENTY-EIGHT

★ ★ ★ ★

The heavens opened and unleashed such a downpour on Daye's car that her windscreen wipers were on maximum as she pulled into a parking bay to the right of the footpath that led to Cranberry Hall. She watched the rain for a few moments before turning to face her passenger. Constable Harry Danvers was mid-thirties and very athletic because he liked to work out in a local gym for two nights every week. He was dressed in casual clothes and a rain proof mackintosh and, although he looked properly dressed for the occasion his fidgety fingers betrayed his nervousness.

'This is the first time that I've met you, Harry,' Daye said in a deliberately friendly manner, 'so I don't know anything about you. Have you ever worked undercover before?'

Harry gave Daye a nervous smile before he replied in a sheepish manner. 'No, Sergeant.'

'Right,' Daye said firmly but not unkindly. 'We are both dressed in casual clothes because we want to look like a married couple bringing our daughter to a dance class. And to that end when we get into Cranberry Hall you will call me Daye, which is short for Daisy, and never refer to me as sergeant. Do you understand?'

'Do I have a pet name for you?'

'No,' Daye replied sharply, 'We don't want to confuse matters. We are Daye and Harry with our daughter Heather. And if anyone asks us where she is she is getting changed in the toilets. Got it?'

'I've got it.'

'Good.' Daye replied. 'Now we go to see Mrs. Honeycutt and you leave the talking to me.'

The rain was still hammering on the windscreen as Daye pulled up the collar of her coat and put on a wide brimmed hat to keep the rain off her hair which she had tied back into a bun. She looked at her watch as they ran towards the entrance of Cranberry Hall; it read 10-37. Most of the parents were leaving the hall and running with their children towards the car park. Only Daye and the constable were running in the opposite direction. The few trees on the front lawn were threadbare and offered precious little protection from the unrelenting downpour.

Once through the big double doors at the entrance the two officers found themselves in a wood panelled foyer which was highly polished and adorned with photographs and certificates. Daye however was drawn towards a shield which was high on the wall facing the entrance. It was a red and white striped design with a ferocious looking black bear standing in the centre.

'That's the coat of arms of the Fitzroy family.' Daye said in a knowledgeable manner but half smiling as she was wondering what it was doing here.

'You're absolutely correct.' A voice said beside her.

Daye turned to face a middle-aged woman, of slim build, dark shoulder length hair and aged about fifty.

'I'm Mrs. Honeycutt.' She politely introduced herself. 'I'm afraid you've missed the dance class. They're just leaving.'

'I believe Mr Buchan has spoken to you.' Daye said in a firm but subdued tone.

'Yes of course.' Mrs. Honeycutt softly replied. 'Please come into my office.'

Mrs. Honeycutt led the two officers into a small office next to the foyer. It was next to the admin office and directly opposite the male and female toilets. As Daye sat in an offered chair, she looked around the tidy room with more pictures and certificates adorning the wood panelled walls. But above the medieval fireplace behind Mrs. Honeycutt's chair was a wooden plaque displaying the Fitzroy coat of arms.

'Can I just ask you a question Mrs Honeycutt?' Daye asked rather timidly. 'But it's nothing to do with why we are here.'

Mrs. Honeycutt looked surprised but answered 'By all means.'

'What's the connection between the Fitzroy family and Cranberry Hall?'

Mrs. Honeycutt smiled and gave out a little laugh.

'Sir Roger Fitzroy helped King Charles the second during his restoration of the monarchy. As a reward he was created Duke of Bellingham and given the Cranberry estate which at one time had belonged to his wife's family.'

Daye smiled sheepishly.

'I'm a bit embarrassed,' she confessed through her slightly heavy breathing. 'I'm a serving police officer in Bellingham and I've never heard of a Duke of Bellingham.'

'Not many people have,' Mrs. Honeycutt said in a not unkindly manner. 'The Fitzroy's died out two hundred years ago and the title died with them. Now shall we talk about why you are here?'

Daye quickly recovered her composure and told Mrs. Honeycutt the plan for capturing the Balaclava Man; she even told her that Mrs. Hanley would be arriving shortly but not with Natalie but rather with a Natalie lookalike.

'Good grief!' Mrs. Honeycutt exclaimed. 'I'm supposed to be taking her for a dance lesson. How am I supposed to do that?'

'You don't need a big hall for one pupil.' Daye suggested. 'A small room with a piano would be perfect.'

'Mr. Redmond.' Mrs. Honeycutt suddenly blurted out. 'His room would be ideal. It's nice and compact and has a piano, and I'll move the women's aerobics to the main hall.'

'Are there any other activities on today?' Daye asked quietly.

'Not until tonight.' Mrs. Honeycutt replied.

'Good.' Daye responded. 'Show us this room, will you? And then we'll get everything set up.'

James was sat in the command seat of the unmarked Police van parked in a delivery bay. He was wearing headphones and looking at a computer screen and was in contact with all the units involved in the operation to capture the Balaclava Man. In the van with him were four police officers dressed in stab proof vests and silently watching all around them for signs of the wanted man.

'Foxtrots one and two are moving into position now ready to block off Duke's Road when ordered.' James spoke sternly as he informed the officers in the van what was happening. 'Foxtrots three and four are already in position awaiting confirmation that the CCTV cameras have found the recovery vehicle from Tattersall's. Deltas one and two are already inside Cranberry Hall and are taking up position. Natalie, one has been exchanged for Natalie two and should be arriving at Cranberry Hall in two minutes.'

'Foxtrot one to Foxhound Leader.' A woman's voice sounded loud and clear into James' headphones. 'Natalie two has turned into Dukes' Road and should ETA at Cranberry Hall in thirty seconds.'

'Roger Foxtrot one.' James acknowledged. He then turned to address the officers in the van. 'Natalie two should be arriving in less than a minute.'

'She's just entering a parking bay now.' A woman police constable sitting in the front of the police van said.

All eyes in the van stared through the tinted windows to catch a glimpse of Natalie two as she and Elaine exited a blue Clio car. Natalie two, Emily, was wearing loose fitting clothes and a long flowing dress that reached down to her ankles. A denim coat and an outsized beret completed her appearance from a twenty-five-year-old to an eight-year-old. Elaine took hold of Emily's hand as they ran through the rain towards the entrance of Cranberry Hall.

'Foxhound Leader to Delta one,' James said into his microphone, 'Natalie two about to enter Cranberry Hall.'

Daye acknowledged James' message. She then signalled to Mrs. Honeycutt who was standing next to the piano in Mr. Redmond's room to go and welcome Elaine and her daughter.

'You stay here,' she ordered Harry 'while I go to the end of the corridor to keep watch on them.'

The corridor ran from the foyer at the entrance to the exit at the back of the hall. On one side of it was the main dance hall whilst smaller studios like Mr. Redmond's room where on the exterior wall on the other side. From her position next to the foyer Daye could see everyone who approached Mr. Redmond's room.

'Good morning, Mrs. Hanley,' Mrs. Honeycutt greeted Elaine and, turning to Emily, 'and how are you today, Natalie?'

Emily did not reply but smiled sweetly instead at Mrs. Honeycutt who promptly turned and led the mother and daughter to Mr. Redmond's room. Daye stood aside in the corridor to let the party of three pass but followed them into Mr. Redmond's room. She then radioed her position to James.

For 45 minutes there was no movement around the Cranberry Hall. Daye was inside Mr. Redmond's room watching out of the external window at the empty car park which was situated to the right of the hall. Inside the room Mrs. Honeycutt was playing the piano as Emily went through some simple dance routines under the watchful eye of Elaine. Outside the room, in the corridor, Harry had positioned himself at the foyer end so that he could watch both the entrance to Cranberry Hall and the whole length of the corridor leading to the rear of the hall.

James was still sat in the command chair of the police van when a male voice spoke into his headphone.

'Foxtrot three to Foxhound Leader,' the voice said with a hint of excitement in his voice. 'Tattersall's recovery vehicle sighted on Manchester Road heading West towards the South end of Duke's Road.'

'Foxtrots three and four,' James replied in his most commanding voice. 'Follow at a discreet distance. Do not attempt to intercept.'

Harry smiled when he heard the message from Foxtrot three. A quick look at his watch told him that in eight minutes time Natalie would be leaving Cranberry Hall and the trap would be sprung. But a look down the corridor disillusioned him a little. No one had come up the corridor except a woman carrying a kit bag who was now approaching him. She was a small thin woman of about thirty with close cropped black hair. Maybe she was from the aerobics group thought Harry.

The woman did not smile or even look at Harry as she passed him to enter the foyer. She was even looking straight ahead of her as she entered the ladies' toilets.

'Foxtrot three to Foxhound leader,' sounded in James' headphone. 'The recovery vehicle is turning off Manchester Road and onto a dirt track which is behind the industrial estate opposite Cranberry Hall.'

'That's an open field there isn't it?' James queried.

'Except for a couple of barns that have been recently erected and the recovery vehicle is heading straight for them. Just wait a second. Let's see what he's going to do. The crafty bugger!!! He's parking between them so that he can't be seen by anybody and certainly not by anybody on the road.'

'Foxtrots three and four.' James spoke into the mouthpiece of his headphone, 'Park up somewhere where you can clearly see those barns and then wait for further instructions.'

'They're closing in.' Daye said in a serious voice. 'The recovery vehicle from Tattersall's has parked up locally.'

'The Balaclava Man is coming for my car?' Elaine stood up and was shaking in trepidation and foreboding.

'You're perfectly safe Mrs. Hanley.' Daye said in her most reassuring voice. 'The police are all around.'

'Don't worry Mrs. Hanley. The Balaclava Man will be coming for me first.' Emily interrupted excitedly obviously relishing the challenge. 'And then he'll be after your car.'

'Aren't you afraid?' Elaine demanded to know.

'No.' Emily replied confidently. 'I can look after myself. And besides I've got the element of surprise on my side.'

Daye could not help but smile at hearing Emily's response, but she was afraid that Emily may be getting too confident and over confidence can lead to carelessness. But the Police would be close by if Emily should be the one to be surprised.

'The aerobics group have left the main hall.' Harry said as he entered Mr. Redmond's room 'time for us to leave?'

'Yes.' Daye replied firmly. Turning to Mrs. Honeycutt she said. 'Will you take Elaine and Emily to the entrance door please? We will follow close behind and keep watch on them from there.'

Mrs. Honeycutt led the way to the foyer escorted by Elaine and Emily; Daye, reporting to James on her mobile, and Harry were close behind. The foyer was empty when they arrived. Mrs. Honeycutt explained that the aerobics group always went to the cafeteria after their workout for tea and biscuits so they would not be leaving for another twenty minutes or so.

The rain had stopped when Elaine and Emily exited Cranberry Hall and began to walk hand in hand down the footpath to the parking bays. Mrs. Honeycutt then returned to her office leaving Daye and Harry stood in the entrance scanning the area for any sign of the Balaclava Man. He was nowhere to be seen. Apart from a few trees on the neatly mowed lawn and some cars in the parking bays nothing was out of place.

'Oh, Jesus.' Daye suddenly exclaimed in horror as she witnessed the Balaclava Man leaping out from behind a nearby car and grab Emily and put a knife to her throat.

Police were suddenly rushing towards the parking bays from the unmarked police van where James was ordering Foxtrot one and two to block off both ends of Duke's Road. Daye and Harry joined the headlong rush.

Emily was not struggling, and Elaine looked frozen in terror unsure as to what to do. As the Balaclava Man pointed the blade towards Elaine and ordered her into the car Emily saw her chance to grab the man's wrist, swiftly bend forward and pulled him over her body to come crashing down onto the ground on his back with his legs wide open. Emily did not hesitate. She pulled her leg back and swung a fierce kick to the unprotected groin of the Balaclava Man who screamed in pain.

He was still writhing on the ground as several police officers jumped on him and firmly held him down. Daye went for his head and ripped the balaclava off his face.

'God. It's a woman.' One of the officers exclaimed.

'Pamela Frankland to be exact,' Daye remarked. 'And you're nicked and so is your boyfriend in the recovery vehicle.'

Pamela Frankland was handcuffed and taken to the police van where James was already ordering Foxtrot three and four to move in and arrest Len Fairhead.

Back in the C.I.D. room in Templegate a lot of the praise for the arrest of Pamela Frankland was rightfully going to Emily.

'You did exceptionally well.' James said proudly.

'As long as I get the reward I was promised.' Emily said firmly and unsmilingly.

'The investigation will begin next Monday.' James replied. 'And it will be led by D.S. Durham.'

Emily said nothing but gave Daye a beaming smile.

'One question I'd like to ask though.' Emily said to James. 'How had the Balaclava Man, or woman, should I say get so close to Elaine and me?'

'Good question.' James responded looking unsure as to how best to reply.

'I think I'm to blame for that.' It was a shamefaced Harry who spoke. 'I saw her in the corridor, but I didn't say anything to anybody. I thought we were looking for a man.'

'We all were Harry,' Daye consoled him. 'And because of that he, or rather she, was able to get near the cars. And to hide behind that car all she had to do was to pretend that she was tying her shoelaces. She was even able to put on that balaclava without anyone noticing.'

'Anyway, they are both safely in the cells now.' James said triumphantly. 'And it's going to be a long while before they're out.'

'Why isn't Elaine here?' Emily asked. 'I know I don't have to call her Mummy anymore.'

Everyone in the room laughed except James.

'I think she found it a bit stressful,' James explained in a sincere manner. 'So, Doug has taken her home. I think she'll be alright. But anyway, well done to everyone.'

As everyone turned to leave the room James called to Daye 'Could I just see you for a minute?'

CHAPTER
TWENTY-NINE

★ ★ ★ ★

James was smiling as he entered the C.I.D. room on a Sunday morning which was sunny and pleasant after the previous day's downpours. He looked over to where Daye was sitting at her desk reading and analysing some documents.

'Good morning, Daye,' he cheerfully said in a jolly Scottish accent which brought a bemused smile to Daye's face.

'Good morning, Sir,' she replied. 'You're in a good mood today. Has something exciting happened?'

'After yesterday's very successful operation to bring in the Balaclava Man,' James began to explain, 'I thought I'd come in extra early to interview Fairhead and Frankland. Unbelievably they couldn't wait to talk to me. They seemed to be in a race to blame each other claiming that the other had deceived them and had set them up for a fall.'

'It sounds like thieves having a falling out.' Daye remarked coldly adding quickly. 'Or should I call it a lovers tiff?'

'They may have had a romantic relationship once, but it looks like this A.V.I.S. program presented them with certain opportunities that neither could resist.' James was looking a little downcast as he spoke. 'And that took the relationship into a downward spiral towards making money by theft, with unspeakable violence, and deception. How could they survive that?'

'But who started it?' Daye asked. 'Surely one of them must have approached the other with the idea.'

'Fairhead has said that Frankland started it by imputing King Kong into the master log when she was at Whittingham Computer Systems.'

James' words startled Daye. She reached for the list of names that Qasim had given her of the Tattersall's employees who were instructed on the A.V.I.S. program.

'Her name's not on the list,' she said in a shocked voice.

'That's because those names are for the people who would be using the A.V.I.S for everyday work. Pamela Frankland would only be dealing with finance. And when she saw that there was little or no protection around the log, she took the opportunity to add King Kong to the user list. She fully expected to be caught but was rather surprised when she wasn't.'

'And she then told Fairhead what she had done, and they cooked up this scheme together?' Daye offered in way of explanation but added ominously, 'and who came up with the unspeakable violence against the women?'

'Who carried out the unspeakable violence?' James asked the question which did not need an answer. He continued 'It was Frankland who targeted the vehicles and Frankland who carried out the attacks. It's hard to believe that a woman would do that to another woman, but the women needed to be traumatised so that they could steal their cars.'

'What was Fairhead's job in all this?' Daye asked quietly.

'Drive the recovery vehicle,' James began to explain. 'Do any repairs that may be needed, change the vehicle's identity and then sort out delivery to the customer.'

'How have you got on with those tasks that I set you?' James said changing the subject.

Daye quickly composed herself. 'All done,' she said with a slight trace of a smile. 'Including the one you wanted doing this morning. It was confirmed.'

'Excellent.' James was clearly pleased with Daye's morning work.

'And you've had a phone call from Dr. Sinclair. When I said you were out, she asked to speak to D.S. Newcastle.' Daye did not look happy as she spoke.

'You two don't like each other, do you?' James said half smiling although he did sympathise with his D.S. He was not keen on Dr. Sinclair either because of her abrasive and patronising manner. 'What did she say anyway?'

'One of the samples of coffee was laced with Rohypnol.'

'I see.' James said firmly. 'Then let's go and see what Miss Anne-Marie De Wynter has to say for herself.'

Anne-Marie slowly opened her front door. James and Daye showed her their warrant cards and asked to enter the house. Anne-Marie said nothing but stood aside to admit the officers. She was stony faced as she led them through into the lounge and pointed to a settee next to the recliner and indicated that is where they should sit. James and Daye duly sat down on the settee while Anne-Marie sat in the recliner.

'Are you alright, Anne-Marie?' Daye asked in a concerned manner. 'You don't look well at all.'

Anne-Marie angrily stood up and faced the two officers.

'What are you two after now?' she shouted at them. 'Haven't you done enough to me?'

'I think that you should sit down and relax.' James said calmly as he stood up and faced the now crying Anne-Marie. 'And perhaps you could tell us what the problem is.'

'I've no job thanks to you.' Anne-Marie screamed at him. 'I've got nothing to do with any murder and now you're going to accuse me of killing Jessica Morris. Why can't you just leave me alone?'

'How do you know Jessica Morris is dead?' James asked quietly looking straight into Anne-Marie's tear-streaked face.

'Well, she is, isn't she?' Anne-Marie said lamely. 'You found her in her car in Hunter's Quarry.'

'How do you know what was found in Hunter's Quarry?' James asked. 'All the newspapers said were that a car with a body inside was found in the lake there. Jessica Morris' name was never mentioned.'

Anne-Marie stood silent and shocked. James could see in her face that she had said too much and was now regretting it.

'Well?' James demanded forcefully. 'How did you know that Jessica Morris was in that car pulled from the lake?'

'Jimmy MacGregor told me.' She suddenly blurted out. 'He confessed to me after he'd done it.'

'When was this?' James demanded to know.

'I can't remember exactly.' Anne-Marie said in an almost pleading manner.

'We already know for certain that Jimmy MacGregor did not kill Jessica Morris.' James was on the attack and was waiting for the right moment to deliver the fatal blow. The moment came suddenly. 'Because we know that you killed her.'

Anne-Marie burst into tears and fell back into the recliner.

'You first gave her a cup of coffee laced with Rohypnol,' Daye said quietly but was still clearly making an accusation. 'It is known as a date rape drug. It first puts the victim to sleep and when she awakes, she has no memory of the attack; except, of course, Jessica did not get a chance to wake up. You took her to Hunter's Quarry where you pushed her car off the cliff edge and into the lake.'

'You can't prove any of this.' Anne-Marie desperately shouted at Daye.

'Yes, I can,' Daye contradicted her. 'The tyre tracks of the car are clearly on the cliff edge and when we searched the car itself, we found your handbag containing two flasks of coffee. One of the flasks contained the Rohypnol; very careless of you to leave it behind.'

'You can't prove that the handbag was mine.'

'Do you recognise this?'

Anne-Marie said nothing while the colour drained from her cheeks as she looked at the polythene bag that Daye was holding. And staring back at her was a white enamel brooch with a shiny silver cross on it.

'How do you know it's mine?' Anne-Marie said in a voice that was barely above a whisper.

'Because this morning I went to see Pat Conway,' Daye replied which caused James to smile with satisfaction. The fatal blow was about to be struck. 'She was your Uncle Jack's sister, and she was with him when he bought this brooch for you for your confirmation. She even helped to write the inscription on the back'

Anne-Marie said nothing as floods of tears rolled down her face. She was lost and she knew it. She walked silently and looked like she was in a dream as James and Daye escorted her to the waiting police car.

The evidence was overwhelming and so she was formally charged with the murder of Jessica Morris.

Back in the C.I.D. room there was an air of satisfaction tinged with a hint of gloom. The murder of Jessica Morris had been solved and the culprit caught. But what about Jack Manning's murder? Knowing that Anne-Marie was behind that murder too was not enough without evidence, but would Benny Gordon ever be able to help get a conviction against her? Only the future knew the answer to that.

'I think we've done enough for today.' James said looking at Daye as she tidied her desk ready for going home.

'I agree,' she readily admitted.

'Then how about another good meal at the Black Bull?' James said hopefully looking at Daye, 'my treat.'

Daye did not answer but her beaming smile did.